"I intend to stay a part of your life."

Jessica looked at the floor, which had begun to spin beneath her feet. "Even if I don't want you?"

"Even if you *think* you don't want me. We shared something special that night, Jessica. Rare, fleeting, almost surreal. Don't you want to know why it happened?"

"I know why it happened," Jessica shot back at him. "It happened because Maddy called off the wedding, and you stayed. It happened because I felt...I felt sorry for you and came outside to...to comfort you, and we got...got carried away in a moment. It was all one great big *mistake*."

"A mistake. I see," Matt said, sighing. "And when you can say all that while looking at me—well, then I'll go away. Until then, however, I'm here. For the duration. Here, or wherever you might run to next."

THE CHANDLERS *Request...*

Dear Reader,

As Silhouette's yearlong anniversary celebration continues, Romance again delivers six unique stories about the poignant journey from courtship to commitment.

Teresa Southwick invites you back to STORKVILLE, USA, where a wealthy playboy has the gossips stumped with his latest transaction: *The Acquired Bride*…and her triplet kids! *New York Times* bestselling author Kasey Michaels contributes the second title in THE CHANDLERS REQUEST… miniseries, *Jessie's Expecting*. Judy Christenberry spins off her popular THE CIRCLE K SISTERS with a story involving a blizzard, a roadside motel with one bed left, a gorgeous, honor-bound rancher…and his *Snowbound Sweetheart*.

New from Donna Clayton is SINGLE DOCTOR DADS! In the premiere story of this wonderful series, a first-time father strikes *The Nanny Proposal* with a woman whose timely hiring quickly proves less serendipitous and more carefully, *lovingly,* staged.… Lilian Darcy pens yet another edgy, uplifting story with *Raising Baby Jane*. And debut author Jackie Braun delivers pure romantic fantasy as a down-on-her-luck waitress receives an intriguing order from the man of her dreams: *One Fiancée To Go, Please.*

Next month, look for the exciting finales of STORKVILLE, USA and THE CHANDLERS REQUEST… And the wait is over as Carolyn Zane's BRUBAKER BRIDES make their grand reappearance!

Happy Reading!

Mary-Theresa Hussey

Mary-Theresa Hussey
Senior Editor

Please address questions and book requests to:
Silhouette Reader Service
U.S.: 3010 Walden Ave., P.O. Box 1325, Buffalo, NY 14269
Canadian: P.O. Box 609, Fort Erie, Ont. L2A 5X3

Jessie's Expecting

KASEY MICHAELS

SILHOUETTE *Romance*

Published by Silhouette Books

America's Publisher of Contemporary Romance

To Ron Hausman,
one of the world's nicest guys!

SILHOUETTE BOOKS

ISBN 0-373-19475-7

JESSIE'S EXPECTING

Copyright © 2000 by Kasey Michaels

This edition published by arrangement with Harlequin Books S.A.

® and TM are trademarks of Harlequin Books S.A., used under license.
Trademarks indicated with ® are registered in the United States Patent
and Trademark Office, the Canadian Trade Marks Office and in other
countries.

Visit Silhouette at www.eHarlequin.com

Printed in U.S.A.

KASEY MICHAELS,

the author of more than two dozen books, divides her creative time between writing contemporary romance and Regency novels. Married and the mother of four, Kasey's writing has garnered the Romance Writers of America's Golden Medallion Award and the *Romantic Times Magazine*'s Best Regency Trophy.

THE CHANDLERS
Request...

Edward Chandler m. ♥ Almira Robbins   † Mrs. Lucille Ballantine

Geoffrey
m.
Marissa Ryan

Ryan
Ruffling Ryan
Romance #1481
November 2000

Jessica
m.
Matthew Garvey
Jessie's Expecting
Romance #1475
October 2000

Madeline
m.
Joe O'Malley
Marrying Maddy
Romance #1469
September 2000

Legend:

m.   Married
♥   World's Greatest...Buttinski
†   loyal Chandler house frau—er, keeper

Chapter One

Walking the beach at dawn.

A time for lovers still dressed in tuxedo and gown, carrying their shoes as they walked barefoot in the sand. Held hands, danced to their own music, laughed and dreamed and kissed as the sun came up over the horizon.

A time for seniors and their metal detectors, cloth bags tied around their waists to hold the treasures of coins and small pieces of jewelry left behind by tourists on this Ocean City, New Jersey, beach. They'd stop, watch the young lovers, smile in reminiscence, then get back to business. The business of occupying their time, settling for smaller dreams, just happy to see another sunrise.

A time for muscle-shirted men and their large dogs: big, playful dogs with names like Fletcher, or Bruno; fierce-looking but bighearted babies who wore kerchiefs around their necks as they challenged the waves, running at them, barking furiously and then wisely retreating when the waves answered back. All while their owners did a few stretches, struck a few poses, admired the way their "pecs" looked: oiled, shining slightly in the light of the rising sun.

A time for a solitary woman to sit on the sand, her knees drawn up to her chin, and watch the mist rise and the sun come up, just as it came up every morning, even when her own personal world had very definitely gone on hold.

Jessica Chandler was twenty-eight years old, nearly twenty-nine. She was tall, with light brown, almost blond hair, for once not secured in a French twist or otherwise tamed by brush and comb and pins—and propriety. Her hair blew against her face in the breeze, hiding her even, patrician features, her tear-wet blue eyes.

She was a competent businesswoman, the middle child of three grown children, wealthy through both inheritance and in her own right. She was unattached, currently on a leave of absence from the company business she and her older brother, Ryan, ran in Allentown, Pennsylvania, and she had come to the Jersey shore to think and to walk the beach.

She was just one more person on the beach at dawn, watching the gulls without really seeing them, digging bare toes in the still-cool sand, sighing sighs the slight breeze snatched away but could not halt.

One of the muscle types spotted Jessica and deliberately tossed a Frisbee in her direction, so that he could shout out, "No, Buster, don't chase it. Be careful of the lady," and then came jogging across the sand to smile down at Jessica, to apologize if his charging dog had frightened her.

The guy was cute, in an overgrown-puppy way. All he needed was a friendly, waving tail and a Frisbee between his too-white teeth. He was tall, with muscles he obviously worked on daily, and had a broad, confident smile. The kind of guy who considered a beautiful woman a required accessory, just like the dog.

Boy, had he ever picked the wrong beach and the wrong girl.

"That's all right," Jessica said, barely looking at him, his handsomeness really not registering in her brain; not considering his attention the compliment he'd believed it to be. Then she stood up, brushed sand from her green shorts and walked away. She headed toward the waves without a backward look as the hopeful hunk shrugged and jogged off in the opposite direction. Buster followed her for a few paces, then grabbed the Frisbee between his teeth, turned, tagged off after his master.

Jessica Chandler was alone on this late-July morning, but she didn't want company, be it male or canine. The very last thing she wanted was company.

Hello, everybody! Bet you didn't know I was here, did you? But I am. Nobody's talking about me yet, so I thought I'd introduce myself. I've been here for a little while now, feeling pretty good, making myself at home.

That lady you just met? Jessica? That's my mom.

You still don't know what's going on, do you? I do. There's a real mess going on, that's what. But don't

worry. Where I come from, there's no such thing as
an unhappy ending. I promise.
Stick around. This should be fun.

The Chandler mansion—the mellow brick building
was much too large to call it a *house*—sat in the west-
ern suburbs of Allentown, Pennsylvania, one state and
a few hours northwest of Ocean City, New Jersey.

Jessica lived there, along with her brother, Ryan,
their grandmother, assorted staff and, until almost two
months ago, her baby sister, Maddy.

Now Jessica's sister was married. Married to Joe
O'Malley, the man she'd left outside a Las Vegas
wedding chapel nearly two years earlier, a man who
had come back nearly on the eve of Maddy's marriage to Matthew Garvey.

Maddy and Joe had purchased the sprawling house
next door to the Chandler mansion. They had just
returned from a ridiculously long honeymoon, and
they were just as happy as they could be—because
the only thing that would make them happier would
be if Jessica had been there to welcome them home.

"I don't get it," Maddy Chandler O'Malley said,
hooking her legs around a kitchen stool as she
watched her grandmother spoon butter-brickle ice
cream into three bowls.

"I don't think that's a requirement, my dear," Almira Chandler purred, licking the metal scoop as she
handed the tub of ice cream to Joe O'Malley and
pointed toward the double-door freezer on the opposite side of the room. "I really do adore Mrs. Had-
ley's day off. Ice cream for lunch. Could anything be
more decadent? At least at my age," she said, wink-

ing one expertly resculpted eyelid—just one example of the several cosmetic surgeries that had Almira Chandler looking twenty or more years younger than nature and the passing of the years had ever intended.

She might be a grandmother, Almira had decided years ago, but that didn't mean she had to *look* like one!

Almira had been in charge of the three Chandler children for more than a dozen years, since their parents had died. And she took her responsibilities seriously, when she remembered raising children was supposed to be a serious venture.

Mostly she enjoyed life and enjoyed her grandchildren, believing that they were intelligent beings and were probably smart enough to raise themselves. They just needed her around to point them in the correct directions.

She'd pointed Maddy in Joe's direction. Oh, goodness, hadn't she ever! She did not consider her actions to be meddling, however. She considered them to be more in the way of *nudging*.

Of course, Almira Chandler's *nudges* could end up sending the *nudgees* reeling....

"Nice try, Allie," Maddy said, giving her grandmother a jaunty salute. "Now, ice cream to one side—and I mean that figuratively only, so pass over my dish, if you please—why has Jessica gone to Ocean City? She never goes until August, when all that fiscal-year stuff is over and she says she can't look at another figure unless it's wearing a bathing suit."

"Besides," Joe said, leaning down to kiss the top of his wife's head, "Maddy expected Jessica to be here to hear all about our honeymoon. Isn't that right, honey?''

Maddy, the baby of the family, with eyes as green as her sister's were blue, and with hair as black as Jessica's was light, leaned back against her husband's strength and stuck her tongue out at him. ''You love it when you're right, don't you?'' she said, then pulled him down for a kiss.

They made a perfect couple: two gorgeous physical specimens who complemented each other in every way. They looked young and in love and happier than might seem humanly possible. Handsome Joe, with his shaggy, sandy hair and cobalt-blue eyes; Maddy, with her wonderfully rounded figure that was such a perfect foil for Joe's planes and angles.

She'd done well, Almira told herself, not for the first time or even the tenth. But that didn't mean she couldn't poke a little fun at the lovestruck pair.

''There goes the appetite,'' Almira teased, taking another bite of butter-brickle, closing her eyes as the confection melted on her tongue.

Joe laughed as he disengaged himself from his bride and sat down on the stool beside her, then looked across the bar at the matchmaking woman to whom he owed much of his current happiness. ''Ah, you love it and you know it, Allie,'' he said, reaching for his own dish of ice cream. ''Mostly because you love being right. Otherwise, Maddy and I would still be pretending we didn't love each other, and Maddy would be married to—''

''No,'' Maddy interrupted, shaking her head. ''No, I wouldn't. Remember, darling, Matt was going to call off the wedding even before I told him I was still hopelessly in love with you, just as I was working up my courage to tell him I couldn't marry him. We never would have gotten to the altar.''

"True enough," Almira seconded. "And now, since I arranged all this newfound happiness you two seem determined to shove under my nose, I think it's a good time to remind you that I'll be old and doddering someday and expect you two to take care of me.''

"A villa in Spain, *high* in the mountains of Spain. Are there mountains in Spain? Ones with nearly inaccessible roads?'' Maddy asked quickly, looking at Joe.

"Is that far enough away from here?'' Joe just as quickly responded. "With full-time keepers, of course, to make sure she doesn't find her way back.''

"And with Mrs. Ballantine installed as head warden, most definitely,'' Maddy finished on a giggle, referring to the Chandler housekeeper, a woman Almira swore she detested—when the two weren't plotting together to run all three of the Chandler grandchildren's lives, that is. The fact that, so far, they'd been outstandingly successful was probably enough to make Jessica and Ryan more than a little nervous. Because if Almira's schemes had worked *once*... well, what was to keep her from trying to improve upon her own perfection?

Not the Chandler grandchildren, that was for certain.

"Not far enough?'' Maddy repeated, frowning. "All right. I guess we'll just have to do it, then. The South Pole it is!''

"You wouldn't dare,'' Almira said, glaring at the

two of them, happy children that they were, friends as well as lovers, and all because she, Almira Chandler, had poked her finger square in the center of their prideful lives and given it a less-than-gentle shake. "Well, isn't it wonderful, then," she said in satisfaction, "that I don't ever plan on growing old."

"Or doddering?" Joe asked, grinning. "You're really going to have to take back that doddering bit, Allie. Especially when you can still beat Maddy at tennis."

"Mrs. Ballantine could beat Maddy at tennis, darling. Blindfolded. But all right. Especially not doddering," Almira said, finishing off her butter-brickle and letting the spoon drop into the bone-china dish with a sharp *clink*. "Now, if we're all done sparring, maybe you'll tell me how the honeymoon really was—and not just a recap of those totally uninformative postcards you sent us for the seven weeks. Let's see, which was my favorite? Oh, yes. 'Having a wonderful time. So glad you're not here.' Hardly inventive, but I suppose you were otherwise involved and couldn't strain yourselves enough to be original. Let's adjourn to the morning room, and you can tell me everything."

"We're not going to the morning room, Allie. We're not taking so much as a single step until you tell us why Jessica is at the New Jersey house," Maddy said stubbornly. "You're much too happy she's there and not here, and I want to know why."

Almira smiled secretly. "You don't have to know, darling. And the one who does have to know anything at all already knows, and the information is probably burning a hole in his brain, straight through his forehead, so that he'll have to tell the other single person who has to know. You two are neither of those two people, but I assume you've guessed that by now. There, now that I have you both thoroughly confused, my work here is done. If you don't want to talk about your honeymoon, I do think Julie could fit me in for a manicure. Toodle-oo, children.''

"But—"

"Give it up, Maddy," Joe said, taking all three bowls to the sink and running water in them. "She's obviously up to her old tricks again. Aren't you, Allie?"

"Me?" Almira exclaimed, pausing on her way out of the kitchen and looking about as honest as a card player with the ace of spades hanging out of her sleeve. "Of course I am, darlings. I'm only surprised you had to ask."

Matthew Garvey laid the last signed paper down on the conference table, leaned back in his chair and sighed. "Congratulations, Ryan, old friend. By paying off this loan two years early and floating that new floor plan account, you've just made the bank's shareholders very happy. Not to mention making yours truly look pretty damn smart in the bargain."

Ryan grinned at his friend, although he couldn't bring himself to quite meet Matt's eyes. Doing that gave him the damnedest, most unexplainable headache. "So, then, I guess you wouldn't want me to diversify. You know, not keep all my eggs in your bank's basket? Divvy up a few of the accounts among the other banks that keep wining and dining me, trying to steal me away from you?"

"Give me their names," Matt growled halfheartedly. "I'll call them myself with your regrets."

Ryan got up from his chair, put his hands flat against either side of his spine, stretched. "Man, one more all-nighter and I'll feel like I'm back in grad school. Jessie sure did pick a rotten time to go find herself."

As soon as the words were out of his mouth, Ryan winced, and not because his back muscles put up a stink at being cramped in a chair for the past few hours. He counted to three, feeling that flash of headache again, hoping to be able to get to at least five before Matt picked up on his stupid, revealing statement. What were such things called? Something close to Freudian slips, he was sure.

And it was all Allie's fault, taking him aside, telling him things he wished he didn't know and then leaving him to do battle with his conscience, wondering if it would be wrong to tell or the greater wrong to keep silent.

The slip of his tongue sort of settled that for him, he decided, still counting silently.

He only got to four before Matt said, "Find herself? That doesn't sound like Jessica, Ryan. She's just about the most complete, controlled person I've ever met."

"Yeah," Ryan agreed quickly. "Yeah, she sure is. Competent…a workaholic here at the plant. She's smarter than I am, in case you haven't noticed. I don't know what we'd do without her."

"But she's gone off to find herself," Matt said, knowing Ryan wanted to change the subject, but holding on to this one small bone of information with all the tenacity of a bulldog.

Jessica had been avoiding him ever since Maddy's wedding—ever since Maddy and he had called off their own wedding, that is, and eloped with J. P. O'Malley, newest king of the computer software world.

He'd called. He'd e-mailed—the communication of choice in his set these days, it seemed. He'd stopped over at the house without notice, on the pretext of seeing Ryan, hoping to find her at home.

Nearly two months now, and she had never once let him close to her. If he came to the Chandler offices, she was in conference; if he arrived at the Chandler home, she was on her way out. She wouldn't acknowledge him; she wouldn't talk to him.

He hadn't even *seen* her since the morning after they'd— Wincing, he tried to rethink the words *morning after,* but they wouldn't go away, couldn't be denied. Just as he couldn't deny that Jessica was avoiding him.

Hell, as far as he was concerned, Jessica Chandler had walked out of his arms and straight into oblivion.

He stood up, walked around the wide conference table. Both he and his friend were a few inches over six feet. Ryan's hair was as black as Maddy's, his eyes the same bright green. And looking as evasive as hers had looked for too many weeks before the now-canceled wedding.

Something was up. Matt knew it. And if the prickle at the back of his neck meant anything, he was smack in the middle of the "why" of the reason behind Jessica's flight from Allentown. "Where is she, Ryan? Where did she go?"

Ryan turned away, peered out the window overlooking the parking lot of the clothing manufacturing plant that had borne the Chandler name for three generations. Almira had been right. Ryan didn't know how she'd known, he didn't know all that she knew—and didn't want to!—but the woman had been right-on in saying that sooner or later Matt was going to come to him, demand to see Jessica.

And now, on orders from his grandmother, Ryan was supposed to tell him. He was supposed to break his solemn promise to his sister and tell Matthew Garvey that Jessica was hiding out—was there another way to say that?—at the house in Ocean City. He had been further ordered to make her disappearance sound as mysterious as possible, then stand back and watch Matt's reaction; tell him more if the guy seemed upset.

Okay. Matt had reacted. And *upset* was probably too mild a word. So how had his grandmother known all this? He hadn't even asked Allie why he had to make the revelation of his burning secret so dramatic. It was one of those things he was certain he was better off not knowing. But he had his suspicions.

Hence his headache...

"I'd be breaking a confidence, Matt," he said, stalling for time, trying to analyze the look in his friend's eyes, trying to tell himself what he saw there was not pain, couldn't be pain. Real, physical pain.

"You're not allowed to tell anyone, Ryan?" Matt asked. "Or just me?"

Ryan winced, not really playacting anymore, because this was his friend, and his friend was hurting. "If you ever decide to sell the family bank, you might want to take up law. You cross-examine real well for a banker. You're right, Matt. I'm not supposed to tell you. She didn't want me broadcasting her whereabouts to anyone, but you were the only one she mentioned by name."

"She mentioned me by name." Matt's eyes flashed blue fire as he felt his hands clenching into fists at his sides. Tension, strain—they'd been his companions for long weeks, and he was almost afraid he was going to lose it entirely and shake the answers out of Ryan if he wasn't forthcoming soon. "And you not only kept your word, you didn't come to me, ask me what the hell was going on?"

"I thought about it," Ryan confessed, rubbing at the back of his neck. "Then I thought about how you haven't beaten down the door demanding to see Jessica whether she wanted to see you or not. She might be wondering that, too. I know Allie wanted me to wait until—never mind. Let's just say I was waiting for the proper moment? God, that's lame. I'm sorry, buddy."

Matt let out his breath on a sigh, feeling his anger drain away to be replaced by something just as uncomfortable. Sometimes he wished Jessica wasn't Ryan's sister. Ryan was a good friend; the kind of guy other guys confided in, told their troubles to, be they financial or female or anything in between.

But the "troubles" with Jessica weren't the sort Matt wanted to discuss with Ryan. Not by a long shot.

"We...um..." he began slowly, searching for the right words. "We, um, Jessica and I spoke together the night of...well, the night Maddy and I decided to break off our engagement. After dinner, when I went out back to the gazebo, feeling pretty much like a fifth wheel at the dinner table. Jessica followed me. Trying to comfort me, I suppose.''

"You spoke together? Out back, in the gazebo, in the dark? Just the two of you? You were gone for a couple of hours, if I remember correctly,'' Ryan said, nodding.

And then he winced, one of his many suppositions reforming into more of a certainty. "Boy, now that explains it. I see it all now. You *spoke together,* and eight weeks later my sister picks up and takes off for parts unknown—at least to you—after spending those weeks avoiding you like the plague. Must have been some conversation.''

"Yeah. Yeah, it was,'' Matt said, going back over to the papers on the table, gathering them up, stacking them neatly. "So was the talk we had the morning after the first one, right before she told me to go to hell. Since I figure I've been there ever since, maybe she'll think I've done enough penance and will talk to me again. Now, are you going to tell me where she is, or am I going to have to tell you things you damn well don't want to know?''

Ryan leaned back against the wall, looked at his friend, saw the naked pain in his usually bright-blue eyes. "I'm going to be honest with you, Matt, because you're my friend, and because you probably should be warned. One, Jessica doesn't want you to know. That's a given. Two, Allie *does* want you to know. Now, if neither of those two facts scares you straight back to hell, I'll tell you where my sister is, okay? The rest is up to you.''

Starting to figure it out, are you? I thought you would.

Now, more about me. It's dark in here, but warm, kind of cozy. And I like the way her heart beats. Slower than mine, but steady, reliable.

I only wish she didn't cry at night.

I'm the one that's supposed to do that, just not yet. First I get to kick her, and maybe give her heartburn. It's a lousy job, but somebody has to do it—it's in all the books. Just so she remembers I'm here, and that she's not alone.

Gee, I wonder how much bigger I have to get before I can suck my thumb....

Chapter Two

Ocean City was a study in contrasts. Billed as the nation's greatest family resort, it was a full-time city in its own right all year-round. But, in with the homes and schools and churches of an everyday town, there were hotels and motels enough for many summer visitors, while the majority of vacationers rented modern condos by the week or the month.

Old homes had been torn down, sacrificed in the name of building the most house possible on the least amount of land, so that the long streets were lined curb to curb with tall, ultramodern condos with fantastic views of the Atlantic Ocean.

Stuck here and there sat stubborn old summer homes that had not given way to progress, small clapboard houses with knotty pine signs over the front door with names like Seaside Heaven or Bill's Dream burned into the wood.

And then there were the grand old homes of some

of the first summer residents, built long ago, even before World War II. These homes near the northern end of the island were more dazzling in their age and design than the most innovative three-floor condo built on stilts and decorated with huge round windows that looked out at the ocean.

The Chandler home was one of these grand old dames. Designed as a Cape Cod, with the third floor built up so that there could be three extra bedrooms under the eaves for visitors, the house was huge, the clapboard painted a bright white. Dark green canvas awnings with white scalloped edges sat on top of each and every window and was duplicated in the large canopy over the huge cement back porch.

Evergreens lined the half-acre grass lot, along with a dazzling living fence of pink and blue hydrangeas that boasted platter-size blooms all summer long. Built-in sprinklers picked up their metal heads twice each day and watered this oasis of green in the middle of sand and cement. A curved driveway led to a separate four-car garage built off to one side, and the rear of the home had a slightly elevated and spectacular view of the ocean that, all by itself, put the value of the home in the millions.

Not that the Chandlers would ever consider selling what had been their summer paradise for six decades.

This was a home that could be picked up and redeposited in Allentown, or any other northeastern town, and fit in as if it had been built on the spot. A solid house. An ageless design, with nothing of the modern about it except for the renovated kitchen and baths, and the addition of air-conditioning.

With two living rooms, a formal dining room, a

book-lined study, five bedrooms on the second floor furnished in cherry woods and oriental carpets, the Chandler house was an anomaly in this resort town, one of about two dozen bastions of a bygone era, and it was lovely enough to make a person weep.

Which wasn't why Jessica Chandler was sitting on the porch, her feet resting on a chintz-covered footstool as the sun rose on another perfect late-July day in this summer paradise, crying into her wholesome glass of milk.

She was so alone. So very alone. Rattling around in this great, empty house she had believed a natural refuge. But it wasn't. It was just a reminder of how alone she was, how alone she would always be, how empty her life had become.

"Because I'm a great big *idiot*," she said out loud before swilling down the remainder of the milk, then making a face at the empty glass. "A great big idiot who *hates* milk," she amended, as she could at least be honest with herself. After all, who was here to hear her?

Nobody.

And that was her problem. She'd told the family to leave her alone, and they'd actually *done* it.

For a lot of families, this would make sense. You ask something reasonable, and they respond reasonably.

But her family? Her *grandmother?* To let Jessica walk away, actually help her *pack*…and then not phone her every day, visit her twice a week, ask her a million and one questions? Her grandmother wouldn't even bother to make up lame excuses for her calls, her visits. She'd just barge in, plant herself in one of the high-back wicker chairs on the sunporch, and say, "Well? Ready to talk yet, or am I going to have to beat it out of you?"

No. Jessica knew it just didn't compute. She shouldn't be alone, even if she'd said she wanted to be alone.

And here she'd always believed her family loved her.

Just showed you how wrong you could be.

Allie was probably all wrapped up in Maddy and Joe, who must be back from their honeymoon by now. After all, even millionaires who owned their own computer software companies had to go back to work sometime, didn't they? Of course, they'd be living right next door to the family home in Allentown, and Allie was probably tripping over there every day, poking her surgically perfect nose into Maddy's business until both she and Joe threatened to put a For Sale sign in the yard...but at least Maddy and Joe had somebody paying *attention* to them.

Why, for all the family knew, she could be lying on the kitchen floor with a broken hip, unable to reach the phone and slowly starving to death. She could have been carjacked on the way down the Atlantic City Expressway, and never even made it to Ocean City. Had they thought of that? Huh? Huh?

No. They couldn't have thought of that. Because no one had called, not in a whole week. Seven days. Seven nights.

She was all by herself. Completely by herself.

That's what being the middle child got you, Jessica decided, heading for the kitchen, letting the old wooden screen door slam shut behind her. Overlooked. Forgotten. Especially if you were a good child, never giving anyone a problem, never making waves, never even thinking about getting into trouble.

She eyed the refrigerator, knowing she had plenty of healthy salad-makings in the bottom crisper drawer. Then her eyes slid to her left, to the smaller freezer door of the side-by-side appliance, knowing that she had a half gallon of double-Dutch chocolate ice cream nestled inside. Calling to her. Singing to her.

"It's a milk product, right?" she reasoned with herself as she headed for the wall of white-painted wooden cabinets and retrieved her favorite bowl from childhood—the one with Pebbles Flintstone on it. "It's just in a more...more *convenient* form, that's all."

In the end she left Pebbles on the counter and picked out a nicely pointed tablespoon, snagged the cardboard ice cream container and returned to the porch. After all, there was no one else around to see her, to want her to share with them. Not that she would, she decided, holding the rounded container close against her as she sat down on the low brick wall surrounding the porch and watched the steady parade of families making their way down the sidewalk on their way to the beach.

Suddenly she was crying again. That was just about all she did these days. Cry. Or think about crying. Or go mop up after crying. If this was what hormones could do to a person, Jessica was definitely in favor of banning them.

Still, it was nice to sit here and look out at the people passing by. The happy people passing by.

She could remember holding Maddy's chubby little hand as they followed their big brother, Ryan, down that same sidewalk, Allie and their beloved Grandpop bringing up the rear, loaded down with beach umbrella, blankets, sand chairs and three sets of sand toys. Even when their parents had still been alive, it had been Allie and Grandpop who'd taken them to the shore, taught them to jump the waves, helped them build sand castles on the beach.

Carefree days. Happy summers. Their fun-loving, jet-setting parents were gone, lost in a plane crash, but as they'd never been around very much, the Chandler children had adjusted well, as if anyone could resist the loving arms of Allie and Grandpop for more than a moment.

Now Grandpop was gone, and Allie was, thanks to the miracles of modern cosmetic surgery, looking younger every year. Maddy was married and happy. Ryan was running the family business and showing all the signs of becoming a stodgy, rather than happy, bachelor.

And Jessica? Ah, she thought, placing her hand over her flat stomach.

Oh, yes. Can't forget Jessica.

Because Jessica, heading for thirty, a hormonal mess with a queasy stomach and her mind filled with notions that had nothing to do with her usual sane approach to life, was about to become a single mother.

She took another bite of ice cream, let it melt on her tongue. Thought about the day she would tell them, tell them all, that she was about to become a mommy.

She smiled sadly. That'll teach them to lull themselves into believing this particular middle child wasn't capable of upsetting an applecart or two....

Matt drove over the Ninth Street Bridge and onto the island that was Ocean City, still rehearsing his lines, rearranging them in his head, mentally striking out whole paragraphs and inserting new ones.

Abraham Lincoln had said more in the short Gettysburg Address than Matt had been able to condense into a near novella of explanations, excuses, sorry reasons and apologies—none of which Jessica would probably give him time to recite, anyway.

And, with all he had to say, all he had to atone for, be forgiven for, he could *not* say the one thing that would get Jessica's full attention.

He had left Ryan's office the previous afternoon and made a beeline straight for the Chandler mansion, dedicating himself to hunting down Almira Chandler and convincing her that telling him everything she knew would be a good thing; that telling it all to him, without prompting, would be an even better thing.

He'd found her on the tennis court, returning serves from an automatic-serving machine being manned by none other than the perpetually black-clad Mrs. Ballantine, the Chandler housekeeper.

Or, as Maddy had more than once referred to the two women: the Good Witch and Morticia, both with Pinocchio noses—noses that were forever poking into everyone else's business.

The two women, Matt knew, made a big to-do over goodnaturedly detesting each other, but he also knew that the pair thoroughly enjoyed each other's company. Even if their friendship was pretty much based on a mutual desire to rule the world—or at least as much of it as they could reach.

That was why he had come, after Ryan had let slip that Almira had told him to tell Matt where Jessica had gone off to a week ago. That one statement had been enough to warn Matt that there was more to Jessica's disappearance than a desire to get away by herself for a while.

When Matt combined that one statement with the knowledge that Jessica was about as conscientious as a person could get, and would never stay hidden at home for weeks on end, or go on vacation while the end of the fiscal year passed over Chandler Enterprises—well, it didn't take a brain surgeon to figure out that something was wrong. Very, very wrong.

Not that he didn't already know most of it, considering he had caused it in the first place.

Falling in love with a woman who, like his own sister, had already married herself to her career, when he wanted nothing more than a wife and family, had been his first mistake.

Becoming engaged to Maddy because they seemed to have shared goals, similar desires for what they wanted out of life had been the second mistake, thinking that being a part of the warm, welcoming, loving Chandler family might be enough.

But not telling Jessica that he had felt relieved rather than crushed when Maddy had broken their engagement...allowing Jessica to comfort him...taking that comforting to a much higher level...well, that mistake could probably win him second prize in the Screwup of the Year awards.

Apologizing the next morning for having made love to her—that had to have netted him first prize, with oak-leaf cluster.

The funny thing was—that was funny *strange,* not funny *ha-ha,* he reminded himself, was that the moment Almira had seen him coming she'd motioned for Mrs. Ballantine to shut off the serving machine and headed straight for him, looking more than eager to talk.

"Darling Matt, it's been too long," she'd said, allowing him to kiss her cheek. The woman was a marvel. Seventy if she was a day, and looking fifty. Acting thirty. Being the best grandmother any three kids could have hoped for: hip, a real friend, and yet still very definitely the person in charge, the person who taught them both love and respect. And not looking at all ridiculous while doing any of it.

"I'm sorry I haven't visited sooner, Allie," he'd answered, offering her his arm as they walked back to the house. "It was probably that No Trespassing sign Jessica put up on the front lawn that kept me away."

"And you should be ashamed of yourself for listening to her," Almira countered, giving his forearm a squeeze as she leaned against him. "But, obedient as you are, you have your limits. That's nice to know, not that I didn't know all along. I have great faith in you, Matt. So, did Ryan tell you where she is? And then let slip that I told him to tell you?"

Matt smiled, shook his head. "I'll assume those were rhetorical questions. I am here, Allie, aren't I?"

"It was that obvious?" Almira frowned, carefully, so that she didn't crease her smooth forehead. "I must be slipping. Either that, or Ryan considers himself to be one step ahead of me. I'll have to teach him differently. But we'll leave that for another time. For now, I'm supposing you want to know what I know.''

"It would help," Matt admitted as Almira let go of his arm, sat herself down in a shiny, black wrought iron chair as he remained standing. "It would most especially help to know if she's just angry, or if she'd like to see me run off a cliff.''

"A little of both, actually," Almira said, accepting a glass of lemonade from Mrs. Ballantine, who then just stood there, her hands folded in front of her, glaring at Matt. He considered asking for a glass for himself, but then thought better of it. The way the woman was eyeing him, he'd be afraid to drink it.

"Oh, just tell him, why don't you. It will be obvious soon enough," Mrs. Ballantine growled, then shrugged her shoulders as Almira smiled up at her. "I'll be inside, running your bath. After all, this shouldn't take more than a few minutes.''

"Such a lovely woman, for a piranha," Almira said after the housekeeper had gone inside. "Now," she said, putting down her glass, "let's talk, shall we? Did you never hear of the word *protection*, Matthew?''

Protection?

What in hell—?

Oh boy. Oh boy, oh boy, oh boy.

Or girl...

Matt leaned forward from the waist, his heart pounding, his eyes all but popping out of his head as he croaked out, "Jessie's pregnant?''

"Bingo! Please select a prize from the bottom

shelf. Unless you wish to play our game again and go for a larger prize?''

"Allie, that's not funny, damn it," Matt said, beginning to pace. Was this the greatest news he'd ever gotten in his life, or the worst? That Jessica was pregnant, carrying his child, was wonderful. Great. Even terrific. But now? Was *now* so terrific?

Timing. Everything was timing. And he couldn't help believing that his timing had been off, way off. No wonder Jessica had run from him. "How..."

"Oh, please," Almira cut in, rising from her chair. "I think we both know *how*. The question is *what*. What are you going to do about it? Knowing that you can't possibly tell her you know. You do realize that, don't you? I mean, I'm not going to have to hold your hand through every step of this, am I? I'm still recovering from leading Maddy about by the nose until she finally saw what was just under it."

Closing his mind to the rest of that short, embarrassing conversation with Jessica's grandmother, Matt left Ninth Street, turned left at the beginning of the beach block, and headed north, on the way to Brighton Place and the Chandler summer house.

Almira had been right, of course. He couldn't tell Jessica he knew she was pregnant. Just as he shouldn't have apologized for making love with her.

And he couldn't possibly confess that he'd been *in* love with her for months...for years.

She wouldn't believe him for one thing, and, for another, he couldn't blame her. He'd made mistakes. He'd made some real whoppers. And now he'd gotten her pregnant—not a solo exercise by any stretch of the imagination—but certainly a result Jessica, the born career woman, couldn't be doing handsprings about, overjoyed.

So, without telling her he'd be there for her, without asking her to marry him, without so much as hinting that he knew she was pregnant, he was here, in Ocean City, without a plan, without a prayer, and with only his stupid, apologetic speech to protect him.

He might as well be going into battle carrying an anchor.

Is anybody else feeling some sort of excitement in the pit of their bellies? Something's coming. Someone's coming. Something's about to change.

Maybe everything is about to change.

And I'm feeling good, feeling really good. Must be some good stuff coming at me now, something sweet and cool that seems to be making Mom's belly happy. Wish I could taste it.

She's doing all the right things. Eating a lot, sleeping a lot. Getting plenty of exercise and fresh air. But still crying too much, and now even talking to herself.

She should talk to me. I am here, right? Yeah, she should be talking to me. I could tell her. Everything is going to be all right. She'll see. I'll take care of her....

Chapter Three

Jessica heard a car pulling into the driveway and held her breath, waiting for it to back out again. The only drawback to living on the beach block was that it was a necessary dead end against the boardwalk, so that lost drivers were forever turning around in the driveway.

She was silly to be worried about a car, silly to think that this car had anything to do with her, that anyone in that car had anything to do with her.

But that was how she'd been, how she continued to be. Jumpy. Sometimes even a little irrational. About as far from her usual unflappable, reasonable, *sensible* self as possible. Wasn't it enough that she was pregnant? Did she have to lose her mind, become nothing more than a supersensitive bundle of over-active hormones and an imagination to match?

It was just a car. Nothing to set off alarms in her

head, set her ridiculously sensitive stomach to doing flips.

Only this car didn't pull out, then head back up the street. She heard the engine die even as her heart leaped into a quick double-time beat. A car door slammed shut.

That couldn't be a good sign, could it?

Maddy? She and Joe were back from their honeymoon, after all. It would be natural for her sister to ignore her plea to be left alone and come crashing in on her solitude.

The solitude that had seemed such a good idea at the start, but that was now rapidly driving her crazy.

It couldn't be Allie. Allie never came to the shore until late September, after most of the tourists had gone home, leaving the beach empty enough for her to enjoy it. If her grandmother hadn't barged in on her within days of her leaving Allentown, she sure wouldn't come now, more than a week later. Too anticlimactic. It just wasn't Allie's style.

Who did that leave?

Ryan? No, not her brother. He had to be swamped at work without her there to help. Besides, Ryan rarely "played." Like her, he was a sober Chandler, somewhat lacking in the fun-loving spirit of their grandmother and baby sister. Working bees, that was what she and Ryan were. Not that Maddy and Allie were drones.

They were natural queen bees.

All of which, Jessica reminded herself, wasn't telling her whose car had just pulled into her driveway.

The process of elimination had left her with one name, one person, and she didn't know if she'd be delighted or angry to see him. If she'd tell him to go to hell or fall into his arms. If she could look at him, remember what had happened—*all* that had happened—and not completely dissolve into a puddle of unrequited love, confusion and more than a little guilt.

Not that she was given time to sort through these possible reactions, for, as she walked off the porch and onto the grass, Matt was coming straight at her across the lawn, looking as bad as she felt.

So accustomed to seeing him in impeccably tailored business suits, she was always rather shocked by how good he looked in casual slacks and knit shirts, both of which skimmed his tall, slim body in most flattering ways. She liked his hair, black as a moonless night, but had never before seen it looking as if he was two weeks past a good trim.

There seemed to be an added purpose in his always confident stride, as if he had come on a mission of sorts, and she wished she could see past the mirrored sunglasses into his eyes, two blue pools she considered to be the window to his calm, cool, collected, almost analytical mind.

But she couldn't see into his eyes. She could only see the tight set of his mouth, the long strides that were rapidly eating up the distance between them. Why, he almost looked *angry*.

Who was *he* to be angry? The nerve of the man!

Jessica tilted up her chin, ready to do battle. She'd give him what for, coming down here uninvited, barging in on her solitude…looking so damn sexy and irresistible.

Damn! Her chin wouldn't stay still; it began to

wobble. Ready tears, always on standby lately, sprang into her eyes, stinging them.

Deserted by her courage, betrayed by her rampantly out-of-whack emotional responses to every stimulus from ice cream to a robin's morning song, Jessica did something brilliant. She turned on her heels and all but ran back toward the door to the kitchen. Safety.

A bolt-hole and denial—they weren't much, but they had worked so far, hadn't they?

"Jessica, wait," Matt said. "Please, Jessica."

It was probably the "please" that stopped her. Either that or the defeated, yet still faintly hopeful, tone in his voice.

Without turning to face him, she allowed her shoulders to slump and said, "What do you want, Matt? Because if you feel some burning need to *apologize* to me again, I have to tell you you've wasted a trip. I don't want to hear it."

The next time he spoke, he was right behind her. She could feel the heat of his body, the warm brush of his breath against her bent neck. "How about if I apologize for apologizing? Would that work?"

Matt winced as he heard his own words, which sounded miles too flippant, even as he meant each word with every fiber of his being. He watched Jessica square her shoulders as she resumed her usual perfect posture, then whirl around to face him.

"Do you know how you made me *feel,* Matt?" she asked, not able to guard her own words or even to remember that they were standing in the side yard, the one facing the sidewalk and the dozens of passing tourists on their way to and from the boardwalk and beach.

"Pretty lousy, I'd imagine," Matt answered truthfully, taking her by the elbow and trying to, gently, steer her back under the semiprivacy of the canvas-covered porch.

She shook off his arm, an expression of temper that was as out of the ordinary for Jessica as it would be for her to chew gum with her mouth open. As if Jessica Chandler had ever even chewed gum. "Lousy?" she repeated loudly. "Did you say *lousy?*"

Belatedly, Jessica realized that they had an audience of three small children and their quite interested mother, who was probably delighted to have some excitement in a day otherwise filled by sand stuck to her sunscreened legs, kids crying because they didn't want to leave the beach, and the prospect of having to wash all the beach towels before returning to the beach after lunch.

Well, too bad. Jessica wasn't feeling much like putting some high drama in the woman's life. Let her find her own and see just how much fun it was—*not.*

Now it was her turn to take hold of Matt's arm, pull him along behind her as she headed for the porch, the screen door and the privacy of the kitchen.

"Lousy?" she said yet again, as the screen door slammed back into place. "You know what? That's the perfect word. Lousy. We made love, you regretted it the next morning, and told me so. How do you expect me to feel about something like that, Matt? *Flattered?*"

"I know, Jessica, I know," Matt said, silently marveling at the sudden color in her usually pale cheeks, the hint of fire in her usually placid, blue eyes, the way her hair swirled around her face.

She looked...disheveled. He'd never seen her disheveled. She looked cute rather than coolly, icily beautiful; and eminently touchable.

He rather liked it.

"If I could have kicked myself all the way here, Jess, I would have," he continued quickly. "The moment the words were out of my mouth I knew they were wrong. Clumsy. I meant to apologize for taking advantage of you, of your sympathy for me...and I ended up sounding like some stiff-necked, jackassed idiot."

"No kidding!" Jessica responded, even while marveling in the new freedom she felt; the freedom to be angry and let him know she was angry. Hey, maybe some of these new, enhanced hormones weren't so bad after all. "I think the words that really put the capper on it were when you promised me it would never happen again. Like, hey, I was sort of drunk, feeling pretty abused, so I grabbed the first woman who offered herself to me, the closest one, and used her. Do you really think I can be *used,* Matthew Garvey, that I would allow myself to be used? Do you know how *insulting* that is?"

Matt opened his mouth to say something and she rescued him, knowing he was going to put his foot in his mouth again by saying "I'm sorry, Jess." If he had said that, he'd be history, out the back door before he knew what hit him.

But Jessica did interrupt him, did save his hide with her next words, words that popped out of her mouth before she could rethink them, edit them into something less revealing. "Well, you know what, buddy,

I'm *not* sorry it happened. I'm not the least bit sorry. Now, what do you have to say to that?''

Matt smiled, slowly, letting the smile pass above his mouth, enter his eyes. ''Thank you?'' he offered, then pretended to duck.

All at once all the anger in Jessica evaporated, like dew on a hot summer morning. ''Idiot,'' she said, walking over to one of the cabinets and pulling out two glasses. ''Want some lemonade? It's a two-and-a-half-hour drive here from Allentown. You've got to be thirsty.''

''It's Saturday, Jessica,'' he reminded her, willing to change the subject for the moment, watching as she retrieved a glass jug from the refrigerator and poured them each tall, cold glasses of pulpy, home-made lemonade. ''I started out before six and I've been on the road for four hours, mostly following minivans with jammed roof racks and bicycles tied to the back bumpers. I guess I forgot that Saturday is the traditional starting date for most people's vacations. But once I found out where you were, which was yesterday, by the way, I couldn't think of anything else except getting here.''

''How flattering,'' Jessica said, handing him a glass, then sitting down at the large pine wood table with her own glass. ''And you'll notice that I'm not asking you who gave you that information.''

Matt chuckled, relaxing even more. He was here, he was in the house, Jessica wasn't killing him, and he might just get to stay. ''What did we used to say as kids? I'll give you three guesses and the first two don't count? Yeah, I'm sure that was it.''

''Allie,'' Jessica said, sighing as she took her first

swallow of the wonderfully tart liquid. She'd had her quota of milk for the day and deserved a treat. "Tell me, did she draw you a map, too?"

He shook his head. "No need. Remember, I've been here before."

Jessica stiffened perceptibly and Matt quickly thought, *There's another old saying you forgot, you jerk. Two steps forward and one back.* Sure, he'd been to the Chandler summer home before today. With Maddy, right after their engagement had been announced. They'd had a fairly large engagement party in this house, as a matter of fact.

"Oh, yes," Jessica said after a moment. "I forgot. Maddy and Joe are back home, aren't they?"

"They arrived the day after you left," Matt told her, trying to pretend he didn't notice the two new flags of hot, rather embarrassed pink in Jessica's cheeks. "Tanned and happy and already tearing into the dozens of crates they'd sent back from overseas. I don't know if their house is going to be Restoration or Victorian England, but they surely did ship home enough antiques to open their own branch of Sotheby's."

Jessica smiled a little at this, knowing her art-history-major sister's tastes that ran from the finest antiques to garish neon lava lamps. "I think we can safely say the furnishing will be eclectic. And she probably sent home a ton of cookbooks and any kitchen gadget she could find. Joe doesn't know it, but he's married himself quite the domestic goddess. I'll bet he's overweight within six months unless he works out."

Then her smile faded as she asked, "How are you

doing, Matt? Is it uncomfortable for you…seeing Maddy and Joe together, that is?''

Now here was a perfect time for the truth. The time to tell Jessica what her brother, Ryan, already had guessed. What Allie had somehow figured out months earlier, so that she made sure Joe had come back into the picture. The perfect time to tell Jessica that he had been about to call off the wedding when Maddy had come to him and confessed that she'd been engaged to Joe O'Malley a few years ago, that he was back in her life and that she loved him.

However, the moment he told Jessica that, she'd have to realize that he hadn't taken—that ubiquitous word—*comfort* from her that night in the gazebo because of his broken heart.

He might have been able to do that, weeks ago. Before those impulsive, heart-shattering moments in the gazebo.

But not now. Not when he knew Jessica was carrying his child.

She would never believe him. She might think that he'd taken advantage of her. The fact that he *had* taken what she'd offered so sweetly, without confessing his love for her, wasn't much comfort to him.

She might even think that Almira had told him about the pregnancy, and that was why he was here now, to pretend to have fallen in love with her, to marry her out of guilt or pity or some other equally despicable motive.

So, knowing Ryan would never betray him, and praying Maddy would keep her mouth shut, he did the most obvious thing. The most logical thing. The most damning thing, but for all the best reasons.

He lied, played the pity card. Shamelessly.

"I'm okay, Jess. I'm beginning to see that Maddy made the right choice," he said, avoiding Jessica's eyes.

Jessica sucked in her lips, wet them with the tip of her tongue. "I see. Always the gentleman, Matt, aren't you? Maddy waited until a few days before the wedding, then told you she was in love with another man. A near billionaire, if the news magazines are right, not that Joe was anything near to wealthy when Maddy first fell in love with him."

She cocked her head to one side, looked out at him from between slitted eyelids. "Joe's money doesn't matter to Maddy. But maybe it matters to you?"

"Jessica, can't we drop this? I don't see what any of this has to do with—"

She raised a hand, waved him to silence as she thought over what he'd said, how she'd answered. And then she got this funny little *tingle* inside her, and her hyperactive feminine intuition went into overdrive. "And you're *beginning* to see that she made the right choice? What does that really mean, Matt? This isn't as if she chose fish over meat or red wine over white. This was supposedly to be a *marriage,* two people in love, remember?"

"We were compatible in many ways, Jessica," Matt answered, backpedaling into truth, at least partway, knowing his words made him sound cold, logical and entirely too businesslike to be a loving groom. "We had the same goals."

"Goals? How romantic, I'm sure. Did you ever *love* my sister, or was she some sort of business deal? Now that she's found a better one, you're beginning to see she made the right move, the right *merger?* That's pathetic! Come on, Matt, tell me. Am I being irrational to begin thinking now that your reasons for marrying my sister were pathetic? That my worry for your feelings, my following you to the gazebo that night was even *worse* than pathetic? God! Does my sister know how lucky she was, to escape your idea of marriage?''

Was she being irrational, as she'd asked him? He didn't think so.

Matt looked at Jessica for a long time, trying to remember that she was pregnant and that pregnant women could be irrational. It was just that Jessica Chandler had never been irrational. She was the calmest, most levelheaded woman he'd ever met. She was even being rational now, in some twisted way—using both her intellect and her emotions to come to logical conclusions that made him look less than terrific.

Yes, Jessica had always been logical, rational. Until the night in the gazebo, when she had shocked him with her gentle giving, her warm passion.

Logical. Until this moment, when she had just about accused him of being a cold, heartless man who'd proposed to Maddy because it made good business sense, without really caring for her at all. Or did she really believe he was that cold, that calculating? Had all the reasons she'd come to him, all that they'd both felt—at least, he had felt it—that night in the gazebo, evaporated from her mind, to be replaced with this low opinion of him?

Didn't she know him at all? Didn't he think he knew her?

He still recognized the Jessica he knew, the Jessica

he admired, the Jessica he had fallen in love with, the Jessica who had her eyes set on corporate success, her all-consuming career.

But here she was, sounding like a woman, looking like a woman—very much like a woman—and confounding the hell out of him as he sought to protect her with lies and damning partial truths he now couldn't take back.

Stupid! Had he always been this clumsy? Maybe the all-American Boy Scout in him just made for a lousy liar. Very well. He'd give her a little truth and then change the subject.

"I'm not going to answer those last questions, Jess," he said finally, taking his empty glass to the sink, running water in it so that the pulp didn't dry out, stick to the sides. His hands shook as he performed the small task. "In fact, I'm not going to say another word right now, because if I do, we're going to have one hell of an argument, and that's not why I came here. I'll only tell you that what seemed like good reasons to marry—to *both* your sister and myself, by the way—no longer seemed quite so valid. Maddy called off the marriage because she loves Joe more than she felt comfortable and safe with me. She's happy. I'm happy she's happy. End of story. Now, tell me which is my bedroom, okay?"

His last words threw Jessica for the proverbial loop. "Your...your *bedroom?* Who said you're staying here?"

He rather liked the sudden squeak in her voice. "Allie, for one. Ryan, for two, and Maddy, for three. As they all own equal shares with you, you've been outvoted. Considering that you'd probably vote against the arrangement, that is. Isn't democracy grand?''

Jessica fought the urge to throw her glass across the room, aimed straight at Matt's head. Being a practical sort, she knew she'd just have to clean up the mess, both the glass and lemonade and any injury to him, and that took a lot of the satisfaction out of such a mad, impulsive gesture.

"I don't want you here, Matt," she said instead, carefully putting down her glass and stepping away from it. "Does that count for anything?"

He pretended to consider her question. "No, I don't think it does. You shouldn't be alone." He'd almost added "at a time like this," but thankfully caught himself before he could shove *both* feet in his mouth. "Besides, since I didn't get to have a honeymoon, I'm overdue for a vacation. I've taken the whole month, by the way. Not a bad job, being the boss."

"A month," Jessica repeated hollowly. "I'll go upstairs and pack."

He let her take three steps toward the hall before he stopped her by saying, "Running away yet again, Jess? That's so unlike you. Totally out of character."

She whirled around, fire in her eyes. "Oh, really! And how would *you* know what's in character for me? You don't know me at all!"

"I know enough, Jessica, to know that you aren't here at the shore for a vacation. You've run away. From me, from my phone calls. From what happened that night. I also know that you can't run away from me, not as long as I can follow you, and, believe me, Jess, I'd follow you. To the ends of the earth if I have to, if you'll forgive the melodrama. Because you and I are going to work this out, one way or the other."

"Work *what* out? You're not making sense."

Matt leaned a hip against the kitchen counter. "I'm Ryan's best friend, Jessica. I nearly married your sister. I've been a fixture in the Chandler house and family for about five years. And I've made love to you in the family gazebo. You and I are going to have to come to grips with that last one, either find a way to put it behind us or take it and run with it, together. Because I am a part of the Chandlers, and I intend to stay a part of the Chandlers. I intend, frankly, to stay a part of your life."

Jessica looked at the floor, which had begun to spin beneath her feet. "Even if I don't want you?"

"Even if you *think* you don't want me. We shared something special that night, Jessica. Rare, fleeting, almost surreal. Don't you want to know why it happened?"

"I know why it happened," Jessica shot back at him. "It happened because you *drank* your dinner after Maddy called off the wedding, and you stayed, anyway, playing the injured but resigned gentleman. It happened because I felt...I felt sorry for you and came outside to...to comfort you, and we got...got carried away in the moment. It was a mistake, Matt. It was all one great big *mistake.*"

"A mistake. I see," Matt said, sighing, pushing himself away from the counter. "And when you can say all of that while looking at me, without having to search for innocent-sounding euphemisms—well, then I'll go away. Until then, however, I'm here. And

I'm here for the duration. Here, or wherever you might run to next.''

Jessica's heart was doing small flips in her chest as she fought not to be heartened by Matt's words. Because he didn't love her, wasn't here because he loved her. He was here because he was a practical man, a damn practical man—a banker, for crying out loud—and he wanted his comfortable association back with the Chandler family, one of his private bank's largest investors.

He wasn't here because he loved her. He was here because he'd made a mistake. They'd made a mistake.

''You know, Matt,'' she said after a few moments, ''according to you, you plan to become a stalker. I think I could get a restraining order.''

''You could,'' Matt agreed, looking straight into her eyes, seeing the hurt and confusion and—could it be?—a slight glow of expectation. ''Or you could change into your bathing suit and show me the beach. I'd much rather play than stalk, and I think I could use some dedicated play time.''

''Between the hours of two and four, Matt?'' she asked, teasing him, somehow falling back into their old friendship, the one that had everything to do with her dreams but nothing to do with their shared reality. ''What about from four to six? Would that be shower-and-get-ready-for-dinner time? Followed by walk-on-the-boards time, watch-a-little-television time...''

''Go-to-bed-alone time,'' Matt added for her when her pale cheeks flared a becoming pink for the third time since he'd arrived. ''Were you describing my day, Jessica, or yours? Or are we both living inside the same box, locked there after years of routine, of dedication, of family obligation, without more than a fleeting thought to who *we* are, what *we* want?''

She would deny his words, except that she knew them to be true. She'd lived her entire life living up to what she believed to be her family's expectations of her. Just as he had spent his, living up to his late father's expectations that had been clearly stated to him, unlike hers, which she had simply assumed.

Jessica wrinkled her nose, something she never did. ''Are you saying we're robots, Matt? That we are going through life as programmed?''

He raised one eyebrow. ''Aren't we? Weren't we? Until that night—that night you can't seem to talk about, much less get past—weren't we both just doing what we thought we should be doing?''

She sighed, felt tears stinging at the backs of her eyes. ''I don't know. I honestly don't know. I thought I was happy, believed I was…content.''

Now was the moment for some truth, some complete, utter, and very revealing truth. ''If we were content, Jessica,'' he said softly, ''we wouldn't have been in that gazebo. Neither of us. Would we?''

She shook her head, waved her hands in front of her as if to push away his words. ''Not now, Matt. I've got enough going on in my life without this. I'm not into Psych 101 right now. Can't we leave personal or mutual soul-searching for another time?''

''Exactly,'' Matt said, grinning, feeling pretty damn proud of himself, even if he hadn't stuck to a word of the script he'd prepared in his head. Winging it, it seemed, worked just as well. Maybe better. Perhaps it was time he abandoned his orderly life and winged it some more. Let it all out, down, or wherever people put responsibility when they didn't want to carry it anymore.

"Exactly what?" Jessica asked, wondering if lemonade and milk were a good combination, or only curdled when put together in her suddenly queasy stomach.

"We'll leave soul-searching for another time, Jessica, just as you said. For now, how about bathing suits and the beach? Do you still have pails and shovels in the storage area in the garage? I think I remember seeing some there. I'd like to see if we could build a sand castle."

"A sand castle," Jessica repeated, seemingly repeating a lot of what Matt said to her as if she couldn't have an original thought. Which she probably couldn't, not with him standing here, smiling at her, acting so out of character that she wondered if she knew the man at all.

Then she smiled, shrugged. "Why the hell not," she said, and turned to go upstairs to get into her suit. It was new, it was the same shade of blue as her eyes, and it fit her like a second skin. She'd bought it on impulse last week in one of the boardwalk shops, one of those aberrations in her usually practical mind she'd been experiencing these past weeks, knowing she'd never wear it in public, knowing that she soon wouldn't be *able* to wear it at all.

Hey, but if she was going to break out of that "box" Matt talked about, why not do it in style?

Are all of you out there getting this? Mom's here, I'm here, and now Dad's here, too. It's about time he showed up, and about time the two of them sat down and talked to each other, maybe even talked about me. Because I'm here now, aren't I, and I'm not going away.

He's told some fibs, she's avoiding looking at the truth, and the merry-go-round they're on is going to go faster before it slows down enough for them to grab at the brass ring.

Parents! How do they manage without us?

There. Don't I sound intelligent? I am, you know. All the wisdom of the world is in me now, as I float here, snuggled in my safe cocoon, caught somewhere between heaven and earth. I'll forget it all, or at least lock it away behind doors that will only open again as I grow up, find my own way in the world. But for now I'm feeling pretty gosh-darn omnipotent, like I know just how this is all going to work out in the end.

Do you want to know, too? I can tell you.

But that can wait, can't it? First, let's have some fun.

Besides, I like sand castles. I'm sure I do. Doesn't everyone?

Chapter Four

If we were content, Jessica, we wouldn't have been in that gazebo. Neither of us. Would we?

Jessica heard Matt's words in her ears as she stripped out of her clothes, tugged on her new bathing suit. What had she answered? Something in the vein of, "Not now. I don't want to talk about that now."

Which was true enough. She didn't want to talk about the reasons she had gone to the gazebo that night, the reasons she had not only allowed the inevitable to happen, but had hoped it would.

She didn't want to talk about that; she didn't want to think about that.

She was much happier believing herself a victim of circumstance, a little too much wine and a perfect, moonlit night.

She most certainly wasn't going to say, "Well, Matt, it's like this. I'm in love with you. I've been in love with you for ages, except you only see me as a very good friend and business associate. So I seduced you. Oh, yeah. I seduced you. Practical Jessica. Calm, cool, collected Jessica. How's that for funny?''

No, she couldn't say that, couldn't say any of that.

So she'd dig out her sandals, grab a towel and go play sand castles with a man who was only here to recapture the "comfortable" business and personal relationship he felt necessary to continue their association.

Talk about your lousy scenarios...

Jessica halted in the motion of bending down to pick up her sandals, catching sight of herself in the full-length mirror across the cherry and chintz furnished bedroom.

Was that her? With *cleavage?* She'd never had cleavage—or at least not enough to write home about, or wear scooped necks to show off. But she had it now. She'd known her breasts had become sore almost immediately after that test strip had turned blue, proving her pregnancy, but she'd chalked that up to overreaction to her situation.

But she couldn't chalk up the way she looked in this bathing suit to some psychosomatic reaction to her condition. She might be throwing up mornings because of it, but she surely couldn't grow her own breasts another size with just the power of her muddled brain, could she?

She stood sideways, sucked in her still-flat belly, admired her body in profile. Her legs were long and straight, and she'd always believed them to be her best feature. Her only good feature, when it came to her tall, straight body, which was so in contrast to Maddy's small, wonderfully rounded one.

Breasts. Son of a gun. She had breasts. Jessica smiled at her reflection, picked up her ecru lace cover-up and headed for the stairs, hoping very much that one Matthew Garvey was about to eat his heart out.

Downstairs Matthew, already in his swim trunks, a towel draped around his bare shoulders, paced in the kitchen, wondering if he had done the right things, said the right things. And he felt like an idiot, thinking these things.

He was a grown man and he was acting like a raw, gangling teenager on his first date.

Of course, there were a few differences: no teenager would have to wade through the minefield of trying to tell a woman he loved her when, only about two months before, he had been about to marry her sister.

What did the English call a touchy problem? A sticky wicket?

Yeah, that was it. His engagement to Maddy was definitely a sticky wicket he'd yet to completely explain.

Jessica's pregnancy? He doubted even the English had a word for *that* one.

He heard Jessica's sandals slap-slapping against the wooden treads of the back staircase, the spiral one that was completely enclosed, with no windows, no natural light. Dangerous steps, he decided in a flash, and no place for floppy sandals or pregnant women.

He all but ran to the base of the steps, to turn on the stairwell light, then stepped back as Jessica appeared around the last turn of the spiral.

He saw her legs first. Narrow feet, slim ankles, not a hint of bulge or wrinkle around her perfect knees.

Legs that were long and straight and went all the way up to...what in hell was the woman wearing?

Matt stepped back, all the way back to those awkward teenage years, and did his best not to let his mouth fall open in typical teenage hormonal shock.

The loose top-of-the-thigh lace something-or-other she wore did nothing to cover up the electric-blue one-piece bathing suit with its French-cut legs and body-hugging sleekness. The flare of her hips mesmerized him as she navigated the last few steps; the slimness of her waist made him want to slide his hands around her, sure he could span that small, enticing area.

He looked higher, having to almost drag his eyes upward, and saw the shadowy cleft between her breasts, watched as her chest rose and fell as she breathed—much too rapidly, he thought, for someone who had simply walked down a flight of stairs.

But it was Jessica's eyes, as always, that caught him, held him. So cool, so all seeing. And yet so blind, so obviously unaware of the beauty that must look back at her in her mirror every day.

Except that this Jessica wasn't the Jessica he knew. The Jessica he knew wore sensible business suits and low-heeled shoes. Blouses buttoned all the way up to the neck. The Jessica he knew pulled her streaked-honey, light brown hair back into a severe twist; she didn't let it fall freely almost to her shoulders. Soft. Warm. Eminently touchable.

Even at home, among her family, Jessica was the formal one, the—for want of a better word—repressed one. The good child. The quiet child who just happened to be one hell of a businesswoman with her eye firmly on her career.

Funny, she didn't look anything like that woman now. She looked as if she'd be very much at home on the cover of some fashion magazine, or she would if only the shadows now in those lovely blue eyes would disappear.

"Ready?" she asked, and Matt realized she'd been standing there for at least a full minute with him looking at her, not saying a word.

"What for?" he asked, his mouth moving before his brain had totally engaged. Then he mentally shook himself, smiled and added, "Sorry. It was supposed to be a joke. The beach, right? We're ready to go to the beach."

Jessica frowned, then pulled her cover-up close around her as she turned away from him, from the sight of his bared chest and the remarkable span of his muscled shoulders. "This isn't going to work, Matt. I know who I am, what I am, and pretending that you've suddenly discovered that I'm more than *you* thought I was isn't going to make any of this easier. Just because I threw myself at you that night and you caught me—"

She stopped speaking as he put his hand on her shoulder, turned her around to face him. "Jessica, that's not true, and you know it. You didn't throw yourself at me, and I didn't just catch you. We met each other halfway, just as we have to meet each other halfway now, try to get beyond what happened and see what might happen next."

"What happens next?" Jessica tried not to look at him, look up into his earnest face, his handsome, adored face and those bottomless blue eyes. Their child would have blue eyes, definitely. Genetics always had its way. "Must something happen next?"

"We can't go back, Jess," Matt told her reasonably. "We can't pretend none of this happened, can we?"

"I...I suppose not," she answered, amazed at the way the heat of Matt's hand burned against her shoulder, drawing her closer to him, closer, the way she would be drawn to a warm fire on a cold winter's night.

"Right," Matt said brightly, stepping away from her. "We can't go back. And these past weeks have shown us that we can't spend the rest of our lives avoiding each other—they have taught us that, haven't they?"

She bit her bottom lip, nodded. "We're bound to see each other at work, and at the house."

"Precisely. So, if you'll pardon my analytical mind, if we can't go back and we can't continue like this, it's time to move on, see what comes next. Are you game?"

Jessica sniffed quietly, shook her head, gave a small laugh. "And going ahead means going down to the beach to build a sand castle? How very illogical. Do the rest of your stockholders know about this rather strange streak in you, Mr. Garvey?"

"Come to think of it, I guess I should be swearing you to secrecy, shouldn't I, Jess? Who knows what the stockholders and board of directors would think if they ever figured out I have a life outside of the bank."

Another thought struck Jessica, out of the blue.

"How…how did the board of directors react to having their invitations to the wedding canceled and their presents tossed back at them?"

"I didn't ask," he said, his mouth lifted in a one-sided smile. "I think the headlines announcing software tycoon J. P. O'Malley's elopement with Maddy pretty much said it all for me."

Jessica sighed, those damn easy tears burning at the backs of her eyes yet again. "She hurt you. No matter how much you're trying to make me think you didn't mind, she hurt you. I'm so sorry."

Say it, part of him screamed silently. *Tell her. Tell her all of it now. Tell her how you go to sleep thinking of her, wake up to the memory of her sweet face, the way she looks, the way she tastes…the way she felt in your arms.*

But his saner part reached up, got a firm grip on him, and yanked him back to reality. The tug-of-war between self-interest and self-protection battled just long enough for self-interest to gain a small victory.

"No, Jessica, Maddy didn't hurt me. We got engaged for the wrong reasons. I wanted a wife and family, Maddy wanted to erase her memories of Joe. Maddy is a born homemaker, someone who needs a house and husband and children, but she also needed to be in love. She wasn't in love with me, even if she might have been in love with the idea of having that home and children."

"But…but you loved *her,*" Jessica persisted.

Okay. Time to leap blindly over at least one small fence to the truth. "Did I?"

"Here we go again!" Jessica's tears evaporated in the heat of her anger. "Well, if you didn't love her, and we're pretty sure she didn't really love you, why did you ask her to marry you?''

Maybe because you never even saw me, darling Jess, he wanted to say, longed to say. And he couldn't say that. It would make him sound as stupid as he felt. "I thought it was time to settle down," he offered instead. What a pathetic answer, even if it was the truth.

Jessica backed up two steps, looking at him in barely veiled distaste. "That's rather cold, isn't it, Matt? I mean, it sounds as if you were *using* my sister."

Matt rubbed at his chin. "And what would you call what Maddy was doing with me, Jess? But remember, in Maddy's defense, I don't think she thought she was cheating me out of anything until Joe showed up at the house. We knew from the beginning that we weren't madly in love, the way the books and movies see it, but we knew we were compatible. We were, and are, very good friends."

He watched as her smooth brow furrowed and she lost herself in thought, pondering his question. "A marriage of convenience," she said at last. "I didn't think those existed outside of romance novels." She looked at him intently. "And—just one more time, because I'm finding this so hard to believe, coming from my baby sister—Maddy *knew* yours wouldn't exactly have been the love match of the century? She *agreed?*"

Ah. At last. The truth! Whoever said confession was good for the soul sure did have it right. Matt relaxed.

"She did. I love Maddy, Jess. And she loves me.

What we weren't, what we'll never be, is *in love* with each other. We were settling, both of us.''

''Why didn't she tell me? I think that's why I'm having so much trouble with this, Matt. Why did she let me think she was in love with you when I—'' She shut her mouth with a snap, turned away from him. Maddy wouldn't have said anything, would she? She would have kept her secret to herself. Just as Jessica had kept her own secrets. Maddy had never known Jessica was in love with her fiancé.

Poor Maddy. Lucky Maddy. Everything had worked out so well for her in the end.

But what about Matt? Did he really mean it when he said what he wanted most was a wife, a home, children? She believed he did, remembering his rather sterile home life, with a career-oriented, much older sister, a driven father and his mother long deceased.

She could see why Matt's conception of happiness was a family like hers, open and loving…why he would have ''settled'' for a marriage that had most of what he wanted, if not the sort of heady, giddy love that, as he said, the books and movies talked about.

Her hand moved to press against her flat stomach, but she quickly drew it back.

It didn't take a rocket scientist to know that if he knew about this pregnancy, Matt would leap at marrying her, finding that wife and home and children. And he probably loved her, just as he loved Maddy. He was a kind and loving person.

But he wasn't *in love* with her. Could she live with a man who wasn't in love with her?

No. She couldn't.

"Well," she said a moment later, picking up one of the sand buckets Matt had lain on the table, trying desperately to remember the latest turn of their conversation. Oh, yes. "I guess Maddy thought it was none of my business," she said, shrugging her shoulders. "And she would have been right. Shall we go?"

Yeah! Let's go! To the beach, to the beach, to the beach, beach, beach!

There's time later for more of this deep soul-searching or whatever it is Mom and Dad are doing while they try to tell themselves that there's no happy ending for either of them.

Fat lot they know! I mean, Hello! I'm here, aren't I? Buy a clue, folks!

Thank goodness my great-grandmother is on the job. Although I wonder how she's going to feel when she finally figures out that she's actually about to become a great-grandmother. Bet that hasn't hit her yet.

Hee, hee, hee. That ought to be fun!

Jessica and Matt walked out across the soft, green lawn, onto the pavement, just as that same young mother and her children she'd seen earlier were heading back toward the beach. Jessica watched, biting her bottom lip, as the woman's eyes went wide, then skimmed over Matt's bare chest, his strong shoulders, narrow waist and long, bare legs.

Eat your heart out, lady, Jessica thought meanly, then remembered that Matt might be a sterling physical specimen, but he was by no means *her* sterling physical specimen.

Still, she felt good, walking beside him, swinging

her sand pail as he carried the oversize, red plastic shovel meant for serious sand castle construction.

And, just for a few hours, just for this single afternoon, she was going to let her heart rule her head and not think about anything else except how good she felt with Matt walking beside her.

"Hi, there," he said to the three children, all boys, who were looking at the shovel, the mesh bag filled with molds and smaller scoops and other sand castle tools of the trade that Jessica's grandfather had collected over the years. "You guys interested in a little castle building?"

"Wow! Cool! Mom?"

Their mother smiled, shook her head. "We're heading to the boardwalk for pizza, remember?"

Three small faces fell. Three small sets of shoulders drooped. And the young mother caved. "You'll have to excuse the boys," she said to Matt. "Their father can only join us on weekends, and I'm afraid I'm not the best castle architect. And then there's this other small complication."

Jessica watched as the woman pressed the flat of her hand against her swelling abdomen, which had been concealed by a bright-yellow cotton caftan. She smiled at the woman, realizing how the young mother's eyes seemed to take on a soft glow. "Yes," Jessica said, "I guess it probably is a little difficult to maneuver."

"You could say that," the mother agreed, then introduced herself as Jan.

"Matt and Jessica," Matt said, also neglecting last names, as this was summer, this was the beach, and who cared a damn for formal titles, anyway?

"Hi, Matt, Jessica. Those three dancing up and down with pleading looks in their eyes are Josh, Andy and Peter. Say hello, boys."

The boys said hello, the whole new group kept on walking until they were padding up the slope of boards that led to the boardwalk. By the time they'd reached the top, it had been arranged that Jan and the boys would find them on the beach after lunch, and the boys would then be put to work on the sand castle.

"That was very nice of you," Jessica said as she watched Jan being pulled along by her boys, who couldn't wait to eat, then get back to the beach.

"Yes, it was, wasn't it?" Matt answered, smiling at her from behind his mirrored sunglasses, still enjoying her flustered embarrassment as Jan's final words hung in the air: "Jessica, you have a wonderful husband, you lucky dog!"

No, Matt wasn't about to tease her by repeating Jan's words. Even if they made him feel good, better than good. "Although," he said instead, "your offer to watch the boys while Jan goes back to her condo after lunch and takes a nap wasn't exactly the act of a socially conscious slacker."

Jessica felt herself coloring, her cheeks turning hotter than even the July sun could make them. "She looks so tired," she said, refusing to believe she felt this instant kinship with the pregnant woman, even if she did. "It was the least we could do. And I do mean *we*, as you're the one who's going to be digging in the sand with them, remember? I think I might just go back to the house, get an umbrella and a book and just laze away the day while you build me a castle."

Matt looked back over his shoulder at her as they

navigated the wooden stairs to the beach, taking the lead in case she tripped. "Fat chance, lady. You're in charge of turrets."

"Turrets? Oh, really. But they're the hardest part. Who decided that?"

"I did." Matt grinned as he took towels and other paraphernalia from Jessica, deposited them on a blanket he'd shaken out, then spread on the sand. "You're the princess, remember? And I'm the Prince Charming coming to rescue you in your turret tower or whatever it's called. It's in all the best fairy tales."

"I see," Jessica said, flattered in spite of herself and having fun, though she had definitely planned to not let him see she was enjoying herself, even if it killed her. "And the boys?"

"Fellow knights of the Round Table," Matt supplied easily. "I've got it all figured out in my head. I did tell you I'm a genius, didn't I? I can add two and two, I can explain trust accounts, I understand stocks and bonds with the best of them—and I make one hell of a Prince Charming." He lifted his shoulders, smiled as he let them drop. "It's a gift."

"And you're a nut," Jessica said, but she smiled as she said it. She bent down, picked up two pails, handed one to him. "Come on, P.C., let's get started before the boys show up. We need to build a strong foundation first, if this castle of ours is going to stand. Grandpop taught me that."

Matt took one of the buckets, brushing Jessica's fingers as he did so, stepping close, too close, and peering down at her over the top of his sunglasses. "That's just what I plan to do, Jess. Build us a strong foundation for our castle. If it takes me all summer."

And then, as she stood there, wondering how he'd taken the conversation from joking to serious in a heartbeat, and wondering why she liked the shift, he bent down, kissed her softly on the mouth.

"I should have checked, damn it," Matt said as he pulled open the screen door and waited for a still-giggling Jessica to precede him into the house.

"Checked?" she repeated. "Oh, Matt, what difference would it make if the tide came in an hour later? The castle was doomed, and you knew it. Although I think I'll always treasure the image of you and the boys digging, digging, digging with your hands, trying to make a moat deep enough to trap all of the Atlantic before it got to the castle."

Matt shook his head, grinned at his own folly. "Yeah, but we gave it our best shot. Andy throwing his body into the breach at the last moment, when the south wall was demolished, was truly inspiring. Jan will be washing sand out of that boy's hair and ears for days."

At the mention of sand, Jessica looked down at her legs, which were covered with it, had begun to itch under the still-damp crust. Matt looked just as bad, with wet and dried sand patches covering him like a leopard's spots. He even had sand in his eyebrows.

And he looked terrific. How could he possibly look so terrific?

She needed to change the subject, fast, before she fell into his arms and told him what a great daddy he was going to make.

"We need to go back outside to shower," she told him. "Otherwise we'll clog the shower drains upstairs.'' Looking down at the tile floor, at the sand they'd tracked in with them, she added, ''And then you can mop the floor while I shower again upstairs.''

Matt slid his sunglasses down his aristocratic nose and peered at her. ''Did I miss the coin toss? Who said I get to mop the floor?''

''Your idea, your sand castle, your cleanup. You can't expect the ocean to do it all for you, now can you? Come on, this sand is beginning to itch.''

Matt tossed his sunglasses in the direction of the counter and started to follow her, then brought himself up short, grabbing on to her elbow. ''Wait a minute. If I remember correctly, the outside shower only has cold water.''

''Your point, you big sissy?'' Jessica asked, grinning at him, making him want to pull her into his arms, crush her hard against him, savor the feel of her sun-warm, sandy body pressed against the length of his. How he loved this Jessica, this happy, carefree, joking Jessica. The Jessica he'd always hoped lay beneath her cool, businesslike exterior and had now found.

''Sissy, is it? Well, we'll see about *that!*'' he exclaimed, dragging her behind him as they slammed through the screen door, headed left, around the side of the house to the small enclosed area holding the old-fashioned shower.

Turning it on full blast, he grabbed a giggling Jessica and pulled her with him under the sharp, cold, stinging spray, holding her there as she struggled to catch her breath, to get away from the water; watching as that water darkened her hair, sheeted down her face, washed sand from her body to reveal her soft, creamy skin and that blow-his-mind swimsuit.

That wonderful creamy skin with the goose bumps forming on it.

He knew just how she felt. This water was *cold!*

"Say *uncle*," he told her, turning slightly so that he was now blocking the majority of the spray with his back. "Say *uncle* and I'll let you go."

"Sadist! Rotten, low-down bully!" If only she wasn't laughing as she accused him. If only he didn't look so very much like Prince Charming, with his midnight hair plastered to his forehead, his sky-blue eyes twinkling with mischief...and maybe more than just simple mischief. "Oh, all right, all right! *Uncle!*"

"Thank God," Matt told her as he turned off the shower, opened the sturdy plastic cabinet housing clean towels. "I thought I was going to have to say it for you." He unfolded one of the large towels and wrapped Jessica inside it, then pulled her close, slid his arms around her, as if drying himself with the same fluffy terry cloth.

Jessica allowed the intimacy, welcomed the warmth of his body and felt herself melting against him.

This, naturally, made her remember that she didn't like him all that much—she didn't, did she?—and she tilted back her head to say, "You can let go now. I'm warm."

"I know, I can feel your heat through the towel," Matt said, still not relaxing his hold on her. "We had fun, didn't we, Jess?"

She looked into his bluer-than-blue eyes, then

quickly looked away. "Yes, I suppose we had fun," she said.

"And started building our foundation?" he asked, knowing he was pushing, but unable to stop himself. "Starting with a fresh base and building on top of it?"

Jessica's heart skipped a beat as her stomach did a small, unsettling flip, reminding her of something Matt did not know, could not know—at least not yet.

She pushed herself out of his arms. "We built that foundation on *sand*, Matt. We both saw what happened to it."

Matt sighed, ran a hand through his dripping hair and followed Jessica back to the house. "Okay, so I'm not so great at metaphors. I'm a banker, damn it. But you know what I meant."

She held open the screen door for him, smiled at him from the dimness inside the cool kitchen. She turned, walked back to him, lifted a hand to cup his cheek, then stood on tiptoe to kiss his mouth.

She whispered her next words close to his ear. "Yes, Matt, I know what you meant. And it was nice, honest. You make a great Prince Charming." Then she stepped back and, as he smiled, visibly relaxed, she added quickly, "And you'll look even better with a mop in your hands."

While he was staring at her, openmouthed, she turned and ran for the stairs, calling over her shoulder, "First dibs on the shower!"

Poor Dad. Mom's sure got him going now, doesn't she?

The thing is, I don't think Mom is all that sure of

what she's doing, either. I reminded her at the last minute, didn't I, just so she doesn't forget me. But she didn't take the hint, didn't tell him about me.

What's she waiting for? What's he waiting for? Can't they see the three of us belong together?

Parents. No wonder they need kids. Otherwise, without having to look at the future, consider something other than their own problems and their pride and other dumb stuff like that, they'd just muddle everything.

But it was a nice castle as long as it lasted.

Next time maybe Dad will use bricks.

Chapter Five

Jessica was still smiling when she came out of the bathroom, toweling her hair dry as she crossed to the closet to decide on her clothing for the rest of the day.

She hadn't brought much with her other than comfortable, years-old summer clothes. Shorts, tops, two pairs of jeans and a couple of sweatshirts if she wanted to go onto the boardwalk at night, when it could be chilly.

Although, she had brought that gray-blue cotton dress with the relaxed fit and small buttons running from the ankle-length hem to the scooped bodice. Light cotton, with the sort of not quite straight, not really full skirt that blew in any soft breeze.

She'd stuck it in the suitcase at the last minute, with some vague notion of walking the beach at dusk, the skirt blowing around her bare legs as she danced in and out of the small wavelets kissing the beach.

Romantic. That was what she had thought, what she'd believed such a dress to be.

Just another sign of her stupid hormones running amok, considering that she had also brought along an ancient flannel granny gown to snuggle in if there was a gray, drizzly day cool enough to make lighting the gas fireplace a reasonable move.

Still, it might be kind of nice to slip into the dress now, over her skimpy bra and panties, with her skin just comfortably warm and pinkish from her day in the sun, with her hair towel dried and allowed to fall free to the top of her shoulders.

Romantic.

She seemed to be very much into romantic these days.

When she wasn't throwing up, thinking about throwing up or staring down at whole milk and broccoli and other assorted healthy foods she'd shunned all her life.

She'd been a good girl. She'd seen her doctor, she was taking her vitamins, she was drinking her milk.

Surely she was allowed one romantic-feeling dress, one walk on the beach.

Just as she had told herself she'd deserved one interlude in the gazebo....

"Damn! Why did I have to think about that?" she asked herself as she buttoned the last of the buttons at the bodice of the dress, then turned to inspect herself in the mirror to see if her newfound cleavage worked as well with the dress as it had with the bathing suit.

"What a mind you have, Jessica Chandler," she scolded herself. "You go from *A* to *Q* to *C* to *L*. Do you even *remember* how to think in a straight line, from *A* to *B* to *C*?"

No, she didn't. Or maybe she didn't want to remember. Maybe she was here at the shore to unwind, to think and to let her mind take her where it wanted to go, when it wanted to go...and without a single thought linked to any sort of order or logic or practicality or any of the attributes she had been known for all these years.

Okay, so she'd go with *Q*, for *question*. Question: *What on earth made you go out to the gazebo that night, Ms. Chandler?*

Jessica sat down on the edge of her bed and stared out the window overlooking the expanse of light blue sky, puffy white clouds and deep-blue ocean. She couldn't see the waves breaking on the beach, just all that limitless water, but the sight was soothing, relaxing. Water as dark as the moonlit night almost two months ago, the whitecaps blown by the wind rather reminding her of the stars that had been in that June sky. Very relaxing.

And, relaxing, she concentrated on her own question. Why had she gone to the gazebo? Why had she followed Matt out of the Chandler house that night? What had she planned to say to him? What had she thought she could do? What had she believed might happen? Hoped would happen...?

The entire night had been one surprise after another. The announcement that the wedding was off. Matt's gentlemanly acceptance of Maddy's decision. Maddy's admission that she loved Joe O'Malley, had always loved him and would marry him sans pomp, ceremony, guests, a reception and the lovely gown now hanging in her upstairs closet.

Maddy's happiness, not to be denied. Allie's triumphant smile, unable to avoid.

And dinner on the table at eight, as usual.

That was what had been so very strange, more than strange. There they all were, having just heard that Matt and Maddy had broken their engagement, and there they still were, sitting around the table, all of them, just as if it was simply another dinner.

Bizarre!

Matt had been so wonderful through it all. Oh, he'd downed a few more than his usual single glass of wine during dinner, but that could only be expected. He'd smiled and joked and let Allie run the dinner that had grown to somehow include Matt's sister, Linda, and Joe's business partner, Larry Barry.

Later Allie had admitted that she'd invited Linda to "prop up" her brother, and Larry Barry because she didn't like odd numbers at her dinner table. Jessica, who used to be able to do simple math before her world had turned upside down, had pointed out that Larry *was* the uneven number, but Allie had only smiled and said, "In your mind, maybe, but not in mine."

Jessica had watched Matt all during dinner, waited for him to say something, anything, that wasn't perfectly polite, horribly civilized. And nothing. He had behaved beautifully.

She knew he had to explode. Soon. And she didn't want him to be alone when that happened.

All right, so that was why she had followed him when he'd excused himself, gone outside, leaving his car keys on the hall table, so that she knew he wasn't going far.

Now, looking back on that night, that moment, knowing what she did now—that the broken engagement might have been mutual, and not just Matt's gallant attempt to make Maddy look less the mean and flighty child—would she still have followed him?

Yes. Yes, she would have followed him, anyway. She would follow Matthew Garvey anywhere, offering her friendship, wanting so much more.

She'd found him in the gazebo, a silly confection of white lattice work with an outrageous domed roof that had been one of her grandfather's favorite follies. Screened in with dark-green screening for privacy— no one had ever had the nerve to ask Grandpop why he and Allie needed privacy at their age—the gazebo had built-in, padded benches on all eight interior walls, and lovely wicker furniture in the center of the polished-wood floor.

Jessica had known the gazebo well, knew every brick of the curving path leading to it through the gardens, as it had always been her "wishing place," her "dreaming place," her escape from her older brother, younger sister, and all her self-imposed rules for how she, the big sister, should behave.

There she had dreamed her dreams, her imagination taking fanciful flights that, eerily enough, had a lot to do with the Prince-Charming-to-the-rescue allusions Matt had, unknowingly, made to her earlier today.

There she had curled up with her feet tucked beneath her, writing in her Very Secret Diary, which Maddy had found one day and taken with her to third-grade Show and Tell.

There she had shared her first kiss with Gary Withers, after the Freshman Sweetheart Dance at school.

There she had studied for school, had her picture taken in cap and gown when she'd graduated from nearby Lehigh University, had sat alone while Maddy blossomed into a beauty and she faded into the repressed, dedicated, very boring businesswoman, whose responsibility was, clearly, to go into the family business with Ryan.

It was where she had come the night Maddy and Matt's surprise engagement had been announced, to cry her heart out until there were no more tears.

How strange that Matt had gone to the gazebo on the night he and Maddy had broken their engagement. How fitting that she should follow him.

He had seen her coming, picking her way along the brick path.

"Jessica? What are you doing out here?"

That had been the beginning. That simple question, and her daring, so-out-of-character answer: "Looking for you."

"Well, looks like you've found me." He opened the screen door and motioned for her to join him inside the screened-in area. "Here," he added, taking off his suit jacket, "you're shivering. It is cool tonight, isn't it?"

Even now she could feel Matt's jacket around her shoulders, the warmth of his body still in the material, along with the special smell of his soap and aftershave. She hadn't been cold; the shivers had been those of excitement, knowing she was where she shouldn't be, with a man who was hurt, vulnerable— and that she didn't want to be anywhere else. "Thank you," she'd said, then turned to face him, put her hands on his shoulders. "Matt, I'm so sorry."

"Why?" he'd asked, cupping her chin with his hand. "Maddy's your sister, Jess, but you aren't responsible for her actions. Always the sober one, aren't you, taking on all the responsibility for the whole family, not that anyone but me has really ever noticed. Besides, I'm all right. Really. This is probably all for the best."

How noble she had thought him! How brave!

How he had *lied!*

And yet, now, looking back on that night, that moment, Jessica really couldn't blame him for his lies, his evasions, his reluctance to tell her the truth. She wouldn't have believed him, for one, and she might have—definitely would have—been angry with him for believing a "comfortable" marriage was better than no marriage at all.

Hadn't he wanted passion? she wondered now. Hadn't he been able to feel the passion in her? Was he so blind to her, that night, the way he had been for too many years? That was what she might have asked him in the gazebo, demanded of him, and then they would have argued, and he would have put his hands on her, trying to get her to see reason, and they would have…they would have…

"We would have ended up lying together on the bench just the way we did, just for different reasons," she told herself out loud, realizing that it didn't matter why they had made love.

They had been destined to be together that night. That was the only logical answer.

A soft word, a softer touch. A friendly kiss that

somehow deepened. Arms that held more tightly, could not find the strength to let go. The dark of night. The moon. The stars. A magical moment in a magical dreaming spot…as unable to deny as her own breath.

A single kiss. Two. A murmured sigh. And then the inevitable.

She had wanted to comfort him, take the hurt from his eyes and grab at a memory that would sustain her through the long, lonely years to come.

"A memory," Jessica said, pressing a hand against her flat belly. "Well, congratulations, Jess. You sure got your memento, didn't you?"

Matt whistled as he showered, feeling pretty good about the afternoon he and Jessica had just spent together, laughing, lugging buckets of water from the shoreline to dampen the sand so it was easier to work with…occasionally "slipping" and pouring those buckets of water over each other instead.

This was a very different Jessica from the woman he thought he knew, believed he loved.

She was so cool at work, with her steel-trap mind for business, her professionalism, her dedication to her family and her career.

She could have been a debutante. She could have dabbled in college, as Maddy had done, taking a major like Art History, with no real aim of ever working in the field. She could have spent her days shopping and her nights at the country club.

But she hadn't. She'd been a business major at Lehigh, just like her brother, Ryan, before her, living at home instead of in a college dormitory, and she'd gone straight into the family business upon graduation, working those same ten-or-more-hour days as Ryan, *more* than holding up her end of the duties.

Just like Linda. Just like his sister, "the doctor," Jessica had devoted her life to her job, her career. There was a lot of Linda in Jessica: the same determination, the same tunnel vision that saw only straight ahead, never having time for a few of life's side roads and the flowers to be sniffed along the way.

Ryan had once told him that Jessica was "married to the job," just as Ryan was. Ryan hadn't said that with any happiness in his voice, but then Matt knew that Ryan hated his job, hated being in charge of the Chandler fortunes—and Matt had been sworn to secrecy after that admission.

So, no, Ryan wasn't happy that Jessica was so devoted to Chandler Industries, although he probably envied her her joy in her chosen career.

Matt just envied Jessica's career, for it received the same focused determination his sister devoted to her own. Neither of them would ever marry; it just wasn't in their game plans for life. Marriage? He didn't think so. Children? Definitely not.

Still, he had asked Jessica out to dinner several times, dinners dominated by conversations having to do with balance sheets and bottom lines and not much else. He hadn't needed a ton of bricks to fall on him to realize that Jessica only saw him as Ryan's friend and a Chandler business associate.

So he'd changed tactics whenever he visited the Chandler house as Ryan's friend. Dressed down, avoiding his business suits. Spent more time on the Chandler tennis court than closeted with Ryan, talking business. Except that Jessica seemed to avoid his company even more at the house, almost seemed nervous, as if she didn't know how to deal with him outside the confines of the office.

"And that's when Maddy came home after calling off her secret engagement to Joe," Matt told himself aloud as he stepped into khaki slacks and pulled them up over his slim hips. "Maddy and her chocolate brownies and flower gardens and joy over all things domestic."

Maddy also knew how to laugh, how to have fun. She wasn't in the least repressed—not bubbly, bouncy Maddy. Even if, upon reflection, Matt now realized that a lot of Maddy's joy was *forced*, as if she was, just perhaps, trying a little too hard to appear happy.

That was what they had been, however, whether they'd known it consciously or not. Two unhappy people looking for any happiness they could find, hold, not watch slip through their fingers.

Maddy hadn't been in love with him, Matt had known that from the start. And he'd never said the words to her, either. Their engagement was something they'd somehow just slipped into, almost without noticing, and then the wedding day came closer, closer, and neither of them knew how to say "Stop! This really is a bad idea."

But somewhere that night when they'd called off the wedding, the gods had been smiling. Not because they'd had a hand in Joe O'Malley's reappearance—that had been Allie's doing—but because the gods had seen Jessica heading for the gazebo that night and had decided on a little mischief.

They'd put fairy lights in her hair, the blush of soft-pink early-June roses in her cheeks. They'd added sparkle to her soft-blue eyes, a hint of vulnerability to her full, unsmiling lips. A bit of daring in her touch.

And then those same gods of mischief had set out stars and a full moon and whispered in his ear, "This is your big chance, bucko. Or are you perhaps waiting for an engraved invitation?"

So he'd taken her comfort, listened to her apologize for all that had happened...and taken hold of her hand as she'd lifted it to press her palm against his cheek. He'd looked deeply into her eyes as he'd turned his lips into that soft palm, telling her without words what he wanted, what they both needed.

"I took advantage of her," he said now, out loud, picking up his damp towel from the floor and flinging it against the nearest wall. "Gods of mischief? The hell it was. *You* did it, and you're not even sorry, are you?"

There was a knock on the door. "Matt? I'm ready to go eat dinner. Matt? Are you *singing* in there?"

He threw open the door, stepping quickly into the hallway. "Singing? Me? No, I was on the phone, calling the office. Believe it or not, nobody's gone to pieces with me down here. Ready to eat, are you? Me, too."

Jessica tipped her head to one side and looked up at him quizzically. "One, Mr. Garvey—it's Saturday. Nobody is *at* the bank offices. And two—there's no phone in that bedroom. Want to try again?"

Matt winced, then grinned. "Busted," he said, bending down and kissing her cheek. "I was talking to myself. All right? I do that sometimes. Me and me have entire conversations, ask and answer questions. That sort of thing.''

"Really." Remembering that she had been doing much the same thing a few minutes ago in her own bedroom down the hall—but not about to admit it—she asked instead, "What did you ask you? And did you answer you?"

Matt guided her toward the front stairs, his hand at her elbow. "Well, me asked, 'What do you want for dinner, me?' And me said, 'Oh, I don't know, you choose.' And me said, 'Me again? Why must I always choose?' And *me* said, 'Okay, we'll leave it up to the lady in the pretty blue dress.'"

"Me—*you* did not! You didn't even know I was wearing a pretty blue...do you really like it?"

"Yes, Jessica, I really like it. You look great," he told her as they headed down the center hall, toward the kitchen and back door. "I really like you," he added before he could stop himself, think about what he was going to say. Before he could think *too much,* as he'd been doing these past years, putting Jessica into slots she might just not fit in, just as he might not fit in all the slots she might have put him in. "I really think we ought to get to know each other better."

"You do?" Jessica walked ahead of him across the grass to the sidewalk, wondering how fast a person's heart could beat before it literally *burst* out of one's chest. "But we've known each other for years, Matt. Years."

"Have we?" he answered, taking her hand, lifting it to his lips, then keeping it firmly inside his as they walked toward the boardwalk. "I don't think so. In fact, I'll bet you don't even know my favorite food. Or movie. Or book.''

"Pizza, *Back to the Future* and anything by Jonathan Kellerman," she answered quickly, then averted her eyes from his shocked gaze as he stopped dead on the pavement. "Those are all just guesses," she added lamely, knowing she had revealed more than she wanted him to know. He must think she'd made a *study* of him or something. Which she had.

"Good guesses," Matt told her as they started walking again. "Let's see. For you, I'd say pot roast, *Titanic* and anything by John Grisham. How close am I?"

"Two out of three," Jessica answered, noticing that their clasped hands were now sort of *swinging* between them as they walked like carefree kids out for a good time. "I hated *Titanic*. I like happy endings."

Matt stopped in front of a shop with a window full of pizzas showcasing every different topping known to civilized man. One of the great things about Ocean City was the number of great food stands on the boardwalk, at least 30 percent of them pizza shops. "You didn't consider the ending *uplifting?* That's what I've heard it called. Uplifting."

Jessica grimaced as she peered into the glass case that was nearly as wide as the shop. "Hardly. The only thing I saw *uplifted* was the bow of the ship, just before it went down." She straightened, pointed to the case. "I'll take the one with broccoli. Two slices."

He couldn't help but see her quickly wrinkled-up nose, and know that she was eating for their child and not her own enjoyment. Leave it to Jessica to jump into any new situation with both feet, fully armed with all the current knowledge on the subject and determined to make a success of it. God, how he loved this woman!

"Broccoli? Well, I can't say I'm not learning something new about you every moment, Jess. I didn't think you liked broccoli, but I guess you're on some health kick or something, right? Me, I'm getting the double cheese and pepperoni, damn the fat calories and full speed ahead."

"I could cheerfully hate you," Jessica told him a few minutes later as they sat in the back of the shop, him biting into his double cheese and pepperoni, her picking at the broccoli-topped dough that didn't even have sauce on it, for crying out loud.

Matt, who had just been about to open his mouth and say something stupid like, "Why is it my fault you're eating broccoli?" instead just smiled and offered her a paper napkin from the container. "Do you want to look in more shops after we eat, or maybe walk on the beach?"

Jessica considered his question, knowing the beach walk sounded romantic, and knowing that he was just being too nice to her not to have something up his sleeve. What that something was she didn't know, but she was beginning to have her suspicions, and they all began with A, for Allie. "I think I'd like to stop in at one of the bookstores, if you don't mind."

Since "stopping in" at a bookstore meant—translated into Jessica speech—spending an hour or more in a bookstore, it was beginning to get dark when they came out on the boardwalk and headed north toward Brighton.

"What time is it?" Jessica asked, looking up at the sky that seemed to be prematurely dark and covered with even darker clouds.

Matt checked his wristwatch. "Seven-thirty. We've got plenty of time, not that I think either of us has pressing business anywhere, do we?"

Jessica shook her head. "No...but it's really dark for seven-thirty. And cool, too, with that wind coming off the ocean," she added, rubbing her hands up and down her bare arms. "Still, nobody else seems to be worried...uh-oh."

"Uh-oh? Uh-oh what?"

"Can't you feel it? The wind just changed. A front from the west has just broken through, pushing the sea breeze out of here. That's not good. I should have checked the newspaper for the forecast."

Now that she'd mentioned it, Matt could feel the change in the wind. It was warmer and no longer coming in off the water; instead it had shifted around, was coming off the land.

He looked at the people walking by, some heading north on the boardwalk, some heading south. And then he noticed something else. Some of the people were just sort of strolling along...but others had begun to walk quickly, definitely with a purpose, a firm destination in mind.

"Where are those people going?" he asked as Jessica took his hand, urged him into the press of people so that they could go with the flow of north-walking people on the ocean side of the boardwalk.

"Those people are either full-time residents or, like

me, have been coming to Ocean City for a lot of years. A quick lesson, Matt. Breeze off the ocean, go play miniature golf. Breeze off the land—*hot, sudden* breeze off the land—and it's time to get the hell out of Dodge!''

By now Jessica was moving very quickly, nearly jogging, Matt's hand in hers as they wove their way through the crowds of foot-dragging teenagers, stroller-pushing parents and gaggles of small children eating cotton candy. "Move, move," she chanted quietly to Matt. "We're only at Ninth Street. We've got a long way to go to get back to Brighton before— damn! Did you feel that? It's raining."

Matt decided he might be dense, but he still didn't see the problem. So it had begun to rain a little: big, fat drops that dive-bombed the boards and the people on them. "It's just a little rain, Jess," he protested as she all but pulled him past a gang of twelve that consisted of six giggling teenage girls and their gangly male opposites, all in baggy jeans and tank tops.

The rain kept coming, hard enough now for everyone to notice, so that the pace of all the walkers increased, even as the wind increased.

Wind whipped across the boards, coming from the land, switching slightly so that it now came from the south, pushing dark clouds and sheets of rain in front of it, both the wind and the rain barreling up the boardwalk like some Mother Nature's runaway railroad engine.

People were calling to their children. Babies began to cry. And everywhere people were running. Running.

And looking back down the boardwalk, to the south, to the wild clouds and oncoming deluge.

Matt stopped, a sea of humanity pouring past him as he stood and watched and grinned.

Jessica gave his hand a tug. "What are you doing?"

"Look at them, Jess," he said, laughing. "Everyone running, everyone looking back over their shoulders. It's every silly horror movie I've ever seen. What am I doing? I'm waiting for Godzilla to rise up from behind the boardwalk, chomping a light post, that's what I'm doing."

Jessica stopped tugging on his arm and looked down the boardwalk to the light poles lining the ocean edge of it, to the masses of people running, yelling, sometimes covering their heads with anything handy, sometimes looking back over their shoulders at the advancing storm.

"Godzilla, huh? Not King Kong?" she said at last.

The rain was coming even harder now, as if the heavens had been lined with water buckets that had all been overturned at once. "Naw," Matt teased her, turning her back toward the north and putting his arm around her as they began to walk. Walk slowly, allowing the already-wet-to-the-skin crowd to pass them by. "We'd need the Empire State Building for King Kong. This is more of a Godzilla set, don't you think?"

"I do," Jessica said, nodding. She was wet, as wet as she'd be if she'd stepped fully clothed into her shower stall back in her bedroom on Brighton. Her hair was plastered to her head, her skirts clung to every line of her legs, even as the wind died slightly and the downpour intensified.

But the night was still warm, and the rain was warm, and Matt's arm was warm as it lay lightly on her shoulder.

She leaned into that shoulder as they walked along; slipped her right arm around his waist. All around them people were still racing off the boardwalk, just as if they weren't already too wet to worry about it. "We're nuts, you know. Everyone else is still running."

"Sad, isn't it?" Matt said, Jessica looking up, watching him as rain poured off his drenched hair, ran in rivulets down his face. "Look how much fun we're having."

"How much—" Jessica couldn't finish. She was too busy laughing. All she could do was keep walking...with his arm on her shoulders, her arm about his waist...and wonder why she'd never before considered walking in the rain to be quite so...so...well, so...*wonderful*.

Hello?

I've been sleeping. Anything good going on? Anything I've missed?

Ah, wait. They're talking. I can't quite make out the words, but they're talking. And laughing.

This is probably a good thing.

Besides, it gives me time to concentrate on me *for a while. I'm supposed to be doing that, you know. Taking good care of myself, getting enough rest. Just like Mom. It sure is nice to rest. Maybe I'll leave her*

*alone tomorrow morning, give her some time away
from the dry crackers and stuff like that.*

*Yeah, that's the ticket. She knows I'm here now. I
don't have to keep reminding her anymore. Next
comes the first kick, but that's not for a while.*

*We'll talk about the heartburn a couple of months
after that, but for now it's about time Mom started
thinking about how wonderful I am...and how much
I really would like having my daddy around. After all,
she certainly seems to like having him around. Right?*

Chapter Six

Matt woke to the sun creeping across his bed, as he'd forgotten to close the windows last night. He smiled, stretched and punched at his pillows so that he could sit back against them, look out on the fresh, clean, rain-washed morning as he remembered the previous evening.

Walking in the rain. Correction: walking in a downpour. Walking with Jessica, arms around each other, letting the rain wash away any cares they might have, any problems that still hung between them.

Coming home to hot showers and hot chocolate dotted with those tiny little marshmallows, a roaring fire in the fireplace and quiet conversation that he wouldn't be able to remember now if his life depended on it.

All he had been able to see was Jessica, her damp hair drying in the heat from the fire as she sat close to the hearth, her long, slim body wrapped from throat to bare feet in a soft, white terry cloth robe.

Jessica combing her hair. Jessica sipping hot chocolate and smiling around a chocolate mustache. Jessica's face, aglow from the heat of the fire, her long neck exposed as she bent forward and combed through her hair, then lifted her head with a slight toss, sending it all away from her soap-clean face, her actually shiny nose.

She looked twelve. She looked her age. She looked like every dream he'd ever had, every hope he'd ever hoped, every wish he had for the two of them even before he'd known he had such wishes held secret in his heart.

How he longed to slip from the couch to the floor, to sit beside her, take the comb from her hand and run it and his fingers through her hair. Push that silken curtain to one side and trace his lips down the length of her throat.

Tell her. Tell her everything. Tell her here, tell her now.

But he hadn't. He couldn't.

So he'd sat on the couch, and she'd sat on the floor, and they'd let the night overtake them, the heat of the fire lull them, and when she'd tried to hide her third yawn, he'd helped her to her feet. Helped her to the stairs. Helped her to the door of her bedroom.

Kissed the tip of that wonderful shiny nose. And left her there.

But today, he thought, rubbing his chin and feeling the shadow of his morning beard, was another day. Today he would find a way, would find the words, to tell her how much he loved her, how much he needed her...how much he wanted the baby she carried.

No. He shook his head, mentally kicked himself. He couldn't tell her that. Not in the same breath, anyway. He'd have to think more about this whole thing, plan some sort of strategy, approach Jessica in just the right way, at the right time. Make her believe, understand, that he loved her, whether there was a baby in their future or not.

Sure he would. And then he'd solve that pesky, cold-fusion problem that was stumping all the world's best scientists.

He threw back the covers, slid his feet onto the floor and headed for the shower. Maybe he'd think better there....

Jessica heard the shower running upstairs and looked at the kitchen clock, amazed to see that she'd been awake, showered and dressed for more than an hour. She'd eaten breakfast. Even better, her breakfast hadn't come back for an encore.

All in all she was feeling pretty darn good. Not as *fragile* as she had felt for the past few weeks, definitely not as queasy. She put a hand to her belly and looked at herself. "Thank you," she said. "How did you know I really didn't want to play the dry crackers and nausea game anymore?"

Then she winced, closed her eyes and listened for the sound of the shower. Still running. That was good. Matt was still upstairs, out of earshot. But she would have to watch herself or stop talking to her stomach at least.

Talking to her stomach. No, that wasn't quite right.

She was talking to the baby. Her baby. A slow smile crept into her face as she lightly massaged her lower belly, as the full realization of the miracle that grew inside her washed over her, heating her blood, tingling her skin.

Her baby.

Matt's baby.

She shook her head, amazed that it had taken her this long to begin seeing her pregnancy as more than that, more than *pregnant…expecting….gestating*.

A baby. She was going to have a *baby!*

Jessica clapped both hands over her mouth to stifle her giggles. A baby! Wasn't it wonderful? Wasn't that the most wonderful thing anyone could think of in this whole entire world? She, Jessica Chandler, was going to have a *baby!*

She all but ran into the living room, grabbing at a cushion on the couch, then she grabbed a second, before turning to face the huge mirror over the sideboard.

Still giggling, she stuffed the first cushion up under her loose cotton top, then the second. Smoothing her hands down over the stretched material, she then turned sideways, got a good look at her profile.

And laughed so hard tears came to her eyes.

Everything else was gone, fled from her mind as unimportant, incidental, maybe even easily solved.

So Matt didn't know. So what? Taking another look at her profile, and giggling again, she decided it wouldn't take him too much longer to find out, now would it?

So she wasn't married. Okay, that was a little stickier, considering her feelings on single parenthood, but something would work out, somehow. Didn't she like happy endings best of all?

The only thing that was important, that *mattered*, was that Jessica Chandler was pregnant, soon to become somebody's mother. A baby. A tiny, helpless, sweet, adorable, wonderful baby for her to love, to hold, to watch grow.

She pulled the pillows out from beneath her cotton top and carefully placed them back in their original arrangement. She'd already had enough frivolity for one morning, considering that Matt would be downstairs at any moment.

Poor Matt. Lucky Matt. He wanted to get to know her better, he said. An optimist could conclude that he had some feelings for her, real feelings, and not just a guilty conscience over making love to her...and then apologizing for it.

Jessica closed her eyes, stuck the tip of her tongue out from between her teeth, and considered that last thought.

That was what had really gotten to her. That he'd *apologized*. That was what had kept her from seeing him, answering his calls. He'd made her feel ashamed of what they'd done, when she hadn't been the least bit ashamed. For once in her life she had gone after what she wanted and had taken it.

She rubbed the tip of her tongue back and forth across her lips, remembering Matt's kiss, remembering that he had come here to apologize for apologizing. Remembering his silly, boyish grin when he had responded thank you, to her when she'd admitted she hadn't been in the least bit sorry for having made love with him.

She hugged herself around the waist, rocked back and forth on her heels. Wasn't he *cute?* Wasn't he *sweet?*

Maybe she'd tell him. News like this was too good to keep secret, after all. A baby. Their baby. After he'd turned white, fainted, picked himself up again, why, he might even be happy about it.

Yes, that was what she'd do. She'd go shopping, get the ingredients for a really good dinner—Maddy wasn't the only one who knew how to cook, darn it—and then later, over dessert, she'd tell him. She'd tell him, watch his reaction…and find out if her happy ending had been waiting for her all along and she just hadn't been seeing it.

If he didn't love her? Did it matter, did it really matter? He liked her. He wanted a home, a family.

She could give him both…and she had enough love inside her for both of them…for Matt, for their baby. Still, it did matter. It mattered a lot, to her.

Matt had taken up what he considered to be his "lookout post" on the front porch, which was directly across from the freestanding garages.

With a glass of iced lemonade on the table beside him and a bowl of pretzels in his lap, he sat in the shade, watched the world walk by and waited, trying to be patient, for Jessica to come home.

Grocery shopping. What could she possibly buy that wasn't already in the vast Chandler pantry, which was so jammed with cans and jars that a gang of about a dozen hungry linebackers could live off that food for a month.

Maybe she was avoiding him, making up errands

to keep him at a distance? She'd left him a note before she'd gone, but it hadn't been anything more than briefly informative: "Gone to grocery shop, be back soon."

When was *soon*? When had she gone? He hadn't heard a car pull out from the driveway, but then, his bedroom was on the beach side, and cars were always moving up and down the street.

He took another bite, absentmindedly gnawing on the thick beer pretzel as he thought over his battle plan. Another day on the beach, followed by an intimate dinner for two at the Tropicana casino in Atlantic City, just eight miles up the coast. There was a great restaurant there right off the casino floor, with a fantastic view of the ocean.

Once they were seated and, after some general conversation and a good meal, when she felt mellow and relaxed, he'd tell her. Tell her everything. Tell her how much he loved her, had always loved her, even when he'd been denying that love to himself, believing it was a hopeless love.

Then he would ask her to marry him.

She couldn't yell at him in public. She was much too well-bred and mature, even professional, to make a scene in public, conk him over the head with the salt shaker or anything like that. That was a very important part of his plan. Personal safety and time to explain. Definitely.

He saw Jessica's car coming down the street and quickly rose to meet her outside the garages.

Although he could handle high finance with the best of them, it appeared he couldn't, when nervous, walk and chew pretzels at the same time. A small piece of pretzel, highly salted, somehow got stuck in his throat, and he was stopped dead by a paroxysm of coughing.

Coughing. Eyes watering. Gasping for breath. He couldn't even swear because he was too busy trying to clear his throat. He turned back toward the porch, running for the glass of lemonade. By the time he'd taken a long, throat-clearing drink, Jessica was already coming toward him, plastic bags filled with groceries hanging over each arm, a five-pound bag of potatoes shoved under one arm.

He ran forward at a trot, still a little off balance mentally, and blurted out, "What the hell do you think you're doing, trying to carry everything in one trip? Why didn't you wait for me to help you?"

He was already grabbing bags from her, pulling at the potatoes. "Damn it, Jess, these are too heavy for you right now, and you know you shouldn't be—"

He shut up, but it was too late. He could tell by the icy-blue sparks coming out of Jessica's eyes that, yes, indeed, it was definitely too late.

She stood stock-still as she held out the last heavy plastic bag—more than held it out...she *shoved* it straight into his gut, so that his breath came out in a strangled *whoosh*. "You *know*. Damn you, Matthew Garvey, *you know!*"

She took a step to his left and started past him, running into the house before he could think of a single halfway intelligent thing to say. Not that there was anything even halfway intelligent he could say.

"I should have just choked on that pretzel and gotten it over with," he grumbled under his breath.

He ran after Jessica, slowed considerably by the

grocery bags and limping slightly because the last bag she'd handed him—obviously filled with yet more canned goods to put in that overstocked pantry—had dropped, landing smack on his big toe. "Jess! Jessica! It's not what you—"

He stopped at the closed front door—the *slammed* front door—both arms full, and shook his head. "Oh, hell," he said as his chin dropped onto his chest just to raise it once more as the door flew open again. "Jess?"

"I've got ice cream in one of those bags, Matthew," she said between clenched teeth. "Ice cream and milk and some horrible low-fat yogurt. And if it weren't for the fact that it's hot out here and I want the damn ice cream, I'd leave you locked out until I could find your car keys and toss them out the window at you."

"Well then, all I can say is thank heaven for butterbrickle," Matt said, trying anything he could to cut some of the tension as he stepped into the house and made his way to the kitchen, leaving the canned goods to their own devices on the lawn. With his luck, they'd probably procreate out there in the sun.

He lifted his arms over the kitchen counter and let three bags slide off his right forearm, two off his left, then dropped the potatoes beside the sink. "Jess, I—"

"Shut up," she said shortly, using a clipped, angry tone he'd never heard from her before, didn't believe she was capable of, frankly. "Just...shut...up and move away from the counter. I have to unload these bags."

He didn't go away completely, just moved a few feet away, taking one of the plastic bags with him as they both began unloading the groceries. "A rib roast?" he commented as he pulled a fantastic-looking three-ribbed roast out of the bag and took it over to the refrigerator. His stomach dropped to his toes. "This was for us, wasn't it?"

She looked at him over her shoulder—*glared* at him over her shoulder—and turned back to the counter, pulling out a bag of baby carrots and some celery.

"Oh, right, I'm to shut up," he muttered, beginning to feel a faint flush of anger rising up inside him. "I'm to just shut up, right?"

She turned her head once more, glared at him again, as if he had just crawled out from beneath a rock and was, in addition, covered with slimy stuff that probably didn't smell too good. The woman could put a whole world of meaning in a single, quick stare, he'd have to hand that to her. "How *could* you?"

Now he really was mad or angry or whatever it was civilized people were supposed to be when faced with a situation at least half of his making and knowing he was at least half-wrong—while feeling pretty sure he was at least half-*right*.

"How could *I*? What about you, Jessica? How long were you going to keep lying to me?"

"*Lying* to you?" She slammed an economy-size box of bran flakes onto the counter with enough force to put some real credence in the manufacturer's warning that the box was shipped full to the top, but may have "settled" during shipment. "I did not lie to you, Matthew Garvey! How could you say such a thing? Oh, this is all Allie's fault! She's the only woman I know, the only woman in the *world*, who could find out I threw up and then go fish a blue stick out of the garbage in my bathroom and *wave* it in my face, for crying out loud.''

Mention of Jessica's grandmother opened a whole new avenue of conversation. It might not be a broad avenue, and far from smooth, but he surely didn't want to detour into the ditch of asking Jessica about blue sticks, so Matt put his mental car in gear and drove straight at it.

''Allie,'' he said, nodding his head, eagerly sacrificing that very nice lady to the wolves if it would help calm Jessica before the next bit of groceries she took out of the bag ended up winging its way toward his head. ''Yes, she really didn't help all that much, did she? It was enough to know where you went, and I thank her for that. But I wish she hadn't told me you were…that is, that we are…the two of us are—''

''Pregnant? What's the matter, Matt, can't you say the word? Pregnant. Preg-*nant*. Go ahead, say it.''

''You're getting too upset,'' Matt said, because Jessica was looking part homicidal, part whipped kitten, and he didn't like to think she felt either way. ''That's probably because you're—''

''*Pregnant!* For God's sake, Matt—*say it!*''

That was it. That was more than it. That was just too damn much. He stalked across the room, took a can of tomato juice out of Jessica's hands and led her over to the kitchen table. ''Sit. Stay,'' he ordered, and went back to unload the rest of the perishables, not saying another word until the ice cream was in the freezer, the milk was in the refrigerator, and all was right with the world—at least the world of perishable food.

"Now," he said, taking her a glass of lemonade he'd poured from the pitcher in the refrigerator and placing it on the table in front of her, "let's talk. No yelling, no slamming of things, no spelling lessons. We're just going to talk."

Jessica's bottom lip began to tremble, and she felt tears stinging at her eyes. Oh, no, she thought. Not now. I don't need a hormone overload *now*. "I have nothing to say to you," she said, then picked up her glass and took a long, cooling drink. "Nothing. Oh, and that sand castle? That walk in the rain last night? Gone! Both of them. Erased from my mind. They never happened."

He looked at her through narrowed eyes. "You think I was *faking*, Jess? The beach, the walk—when I kissed you? When you kissed me back? You think it was all a put-on, because Allie told me you're pregnant? You think I'm that *low?*"

No, she didn't. "Yes, I do," she declared, lifting her chin defiantly. "I think you're here on orders from Allie, to make an honest woman out of me. And it shouldn't be too much of a stretch for you, Matt. After all, if you weren't in love with Maddy, it doesn't matter that you're not in love with me. Just another convenient Chandler to give you that home and family you want so much."

Matt rubbed a hand across his mouth, doing his best not to explode, to say something that would make it impossible for them to ever reach an understanding, let alone have a chance for a future together, one where he could try to make it up to her for having put a crimp in her career plans, if that was how she saw this pregnancy. Because he really didn't know how she did see this pregnancy. Not at all. He sure hadn't seen any knitting needles or little blue bootees lying around, had he?

"I'm not going to give you some sob story about my lonely upbringing as an only child with no mother, Jessica, living with a father who might have loved me but saw me as more of a replacement to train to take over the bank when he was gone. I'm just not going to go there, say anything more than I've just said, because it's *my* life, Jess, and I'm not going to apologize for it, or for what I want out of life, what I want for my children."

"Matt, I—" Jessica began, feeling suddenly ashamed of herself. She knew about Matt's background, his lack of a loving home. She knew that was why he had been so attracted to the happy, laughing, loving, fairly irreverent Chandler clan as ruled by their own Auntie Mame of a grandmother. "I'm sorry…I shouldn't have…that was really cruel of me, and—"

He waved off her apology. "Forget it," he said, getting up from his chair to begin pacing the kitchen.

Jessica sat very still, tracing a fingertip down the side of the frosted glass, following the drip of condensation as the ice began to melt. There was nothing else to say, nothing else to do.

"All right," Matt said after a few oppressively silent minutes. He walked back over to the table and put his hands, and his deal, on that table as he looked into her eyes. "This is how it goes. We made love, you got pregnant, we get married. Not today, because there's a license to get and maybe blood tests if they do them here in New Jersey—I have no idea. Three days, Jessica, that's about all it takes. Three days, and the two of us get married. No big to-do, no reception for 350 of our closest friends. Just you and me and the minister of your choice. You do have a minister, a church down here you attend during the summer, don't you?''

Married? He'd actually said that word *married?* After the way they'd been tearing at each other, yelling at each other? Jessica was so taken aback that she actually answered him. "Reverend Colter. I'm sure he—wait a minute! Who says we're getting married?''

"I do, Jess. You're carrying my child, and my child is going to carry my name. I'm going to support him, be there for him, be there for you. If you want to go back to the offices, fine, we'll hire a nanny. But I'm going to be in this child's life, Jessica, not just another absentee dad, visiting him every other weekend. Understand?''

She bent her head, nodding. They were right back to square one, the part where she had a problem, and he, out of the goodness of his heart, was going to solve it. "The child. Of course. You want what's best for the child. That's understandable.'' No words of love, not so much as a kiss on her cheek. Nothing. Just the child, whom he seemed to believe she didn't even really want all that badly, if he thought she was going to rush straight back to Chandler Industries and her career.

So much for sand castles, walks in the rain, soft

kisses that could mean anything or, as it turned out, nothing.

How could he have known her all these years and never realized that her career was a substitute for a life, that she had taken on the responsibility the same way Ryan had, because she'd felt it was expected of her when their parents died? Had he felt nothing but some ridiculous release of tension that night they'd made love? Had he felt nothing last night, as they walked the boardwalk arm in arm in the rain?

Obviously not. And that "getting to know each other better" was all just something to say, some way to get himself invited to stay here until he could tell her he knew about the baby and wanted to marry her to be close to that baby.

She'd actually begun to hope…to think—but, no. She couldn't think that way.

Matt reached out a hand, came within a whisper of touching her bent head and then retreated. He loved her so much, and if he told her that now, she'd probably feel justified in killing him. "It's going to be all right, Jess. We can be happy."

"Happy," she repeated hollowly. "Yes, of course."

Well, I don't know about you guys, but I'm bummed.

Dad isn't exactly the last of the great romantics, is he? As a matter of fact, he was pretty bad. Really bad. Pathetic.

Mom's mad. Man, is she mad! Mad and crying and hiding out in our bedroom eating a whole bag of chocolate candies she really shouldn't be eating, while Dad's out looking up this Reverend Colter guy and finding out where to get a license.

You need a license to be married, to be parents? I didn't know that. But it's probably a good idea.

Although I think Mom and Dad are going to have to do some heavy cramming if they want to pass the final exam and get that license!

Yeah, well, back to work. I've gotta keep growing, keep chowing down everything Mom sends me. Moving around a little, feeling my heart beat. I like to feel my heart beat. I think I'm getting pretty good at this fetus stuff, actually.

Hey! Look! That's my thumb! I think...maybe... yes...I can just get it into my—darn!

Okay, so does anybody out there know how to get a thumb out of an ear?

Chapter Seven

"Chandler here."

Matt held one hand over his ear as a family pedaling a four-seater buggy went by on the boardwalk. "Ryan?"

"Hello?"

"Ryan, it's me. Matt."

There was a five-second silence, followed by "Matt? Do I know a Matt? Do you have a last name? Where did we meet? Maybe if you described yourself?"

"Very funny, Ryan," Matt all but yelled into his cell phone as he walked down a short flight of wooden steps, onto the relative quiet of the beach. "I know I said I'd call—"

"*Au contraire*, Matthew, as Allie might say," Ryan interrupted. "You *promised* you'd call—there's a difference. And, if you couldn't call, couldn't you at least have kept your cell phone turned on? Or did you think I'd take the chance of phoning the house and having Jessica answer—at which point she'd figuratively rip my head clean off my shoulders, in case you haven't figured that one out for yourself.''

"I know, I know—"

"Don't interrupt. I've been waiting to yell at you, and I think I'm on a roll," Ryan warned. "Then there's the matter of one Almira Chandler. Remember her, Matt? I do. I can hardly forget, considering that, heaven help me, she sees me as a sort of coconspirator in this one. She expects reports, results, and she expects them *yesterday*, Matthew. I'm hiding here in the office twelve hours a day, ducking phone calls from my own grandmother. She'll be here soon. I know it and I can't get my secretary to agree to help me push all the furniture against my office door to keep Allie out. That being said, do you have any news for me? Because, if you don't, I really don't want to talk to you. I'll be too busy packing for my escape to the hills somewhere.''

Matt had held the slim silver phone away from his ear halfway through Ryan's verbal explosion, partially stunned by his friend's half serious, half way-too-chipper voice; the rest of him wondering what in hell he could tell Matt that wouldn't have Allie Chandler, probably with Mrs. Ballantine in tow, swooping down on Ocean City on the next chauffeured broom.

"Can't we keep Allie out of this?" he said, when it appeared Ryan was finished. "I mean, I adore Allie, I really do…just not right now."

There was another short, heavy pause. "Do you know how to stop a herd of runaway horses, Matt?"

Matt winced. "No."

"Then I don't think you can stop her," Ryan said, chuckling. "Seriously, Matt, I can only hold the woman off so long and, to tell you the truth, I don't think I'm really holding her off at all. I think she's just humoring me while she makes other plans. But if you've got something for me? Something I can use to head her off a while longer?"

"Oh, I've got something all right," Matt said, smiling at a toddler who had somehow come to be standing in front of him, holding up a small plastic pail as if asking him to join him, come play with him. "Not now, sweetheart," he said, forgetting to cover the phone.

"*Not now, sweetheart?* For crying out loud, Matt, is Jessica there with you? Have you told her what you told me? Is everything just hunky-dory fine between you, while I'm here fighting the battle of the advancing Almira Army? That's not playing fair, friend."

The little toddler, all big blue eyes and blowing blond curls, frowned mightily and, without warning, dumped the contents of his small plastic pail right on Matt's sneakers; contents consisting of sea water, sand and half a dead horseshoe crab. He then giggled, turned on his little bare feet and chugged away on sturdy little legs—a cherub gone bad at the age of three. "Damn it!"

"Damn *what?*" Ryan asked from the other end of the wireless line, obviously more confused now than angry, although both emotions were fighting each other for dominance. "Matt? Is Jessica with you or not?"

Sitting down on the end of the wooden steps in

order to pull off his sopping sneakers, Matt asked, "Would that be in mind, spirit or body, Ryan?"

"Pick one, any one. You came to my office, told me you and Jessica…that you and Jess—aw, hell, you know what you told me. And you also told me you love Jessica, have loved Jessica for a long time—I'm still working it out in my head why the hell you didn't tell *her* that—and then you went down to the beach house, prepared to lay siege until Jessica told you whatever the hell it is Allie already told you but, damn it, won't tell me. Now, Matthew, old friend, old buddy, I'm left to wonder if I should help you, sic Allie on you or come down there myself and punch you in the nose. For about the twelfth and definitely last time, *what's going on?*"

Matt took a deep breath, let it out slowly and began, "I drove down to the house. Jess wasn't happy to see me, but then I worked my massive Garvey charm on her—that's a joke, Ryan—and she didn't throw me out on my ear. We were getting on great until I let it slip that I know she's pregnant—"

Ryan interrupted with a few unrepeatable words that had Matt wincing, knowing his good friend had every right to say whatever came into his mind and out his mouth.

"So, I guess this means you weren't kidding, and Allie didn't tell you what she told me?" Matt offered, wincing again.

"Pregnant? My sister's *pregnant?* For God's sake, Matt, a couple of months ago—is it even three months yet? No, it isn't!—you were about to marry Maddy. And now you're telling me Jess is *pregnant?* What the hell's the *matter* with you?"

Holding on to his sneakers with one hand, the phone with the other, Matt began walking up the beach, toward Brighton and the beach house. "One, Ryan, I never touched Maddy. It wasn't that kind of relationship, which is one of the nine hundred reasons we never should have become engaged in the first place."

"Yeah, well, I know that," Ryan answered. "But that doesn't mean the rest of the world would believe it. How could you get my sisters into this mess?"

Matt stopped dead, Ryan's words finally making him begin to see the entire situation from the outside, from anyone else's point of view and not just his own. "Do you think Jessica thinks that way?" he asked. "Do you think she's *embarrassed,* afraid to show her face back in Allentown? Damn, Ryan, I never even thought of that."

"You haven't been thinking about much of anything, old friend, in my opinion. But if Maddy can dump you—that's also in the eyes of the world or society or whatever—I suppose you marrying Jess a couple months later isn't exactly going to make anyone think it's anything more than another crazy Chandler thing, something they've all come to expect, considering Allie raised us. And everyone knows Almira Chandler is nice enough but has more than a couple of loose screws rattling around in her head."

"She does not, Ryan," Matt said, finding himself defending Jessica's grandmother. "Allie's one of the brightest, funniest, smartest women I've ever met."

"Hey, don't yell at me, friend, I know that. You know that. Our whole family knows that. But you have to admit she's gone a little overboard on the cosmetic-surgery thing, the beating-women-thirty-years-younger-at-tennis thing, the dance-all-night-and-know-all-the-latest-dances thing, the cherry-red-convertible-sports-car thing—I could go on, but what's the point? Allie's Allie, and we adore her, end of story. Allie's story. But now, let's get back to Jessica and Matt's story, shall we?''

Matt would rather seek out the pail-carrying toddler and ask him to dump its contents over his head this time, but he sucked it up and agreed. ''All right, Ryan. Back to Jess and me. She's not with me, by the way, which I suppose you already figured out for yourself, or else this conversation would have been over the moment she heard you yell the word *pregnant* and she'd have grabbed the phone from me to tell you where you could go with that new knowledge.''

''Actually, I think I hear seagulls and waves crashing on the beach,'' Ryan said honestly. ''These new phones are something else. In another moment I'll think I can smell the salt in the air.''

Matt chuckled. ''Yeah, I'm on the beach, having just come back from a quite nice talk with Reverend Colter, who has agreed to marry Jess and me this coming Saturday morning, right here on this same beach. That sounds highly romantic, Ryan, until, one, I tell you that the church is booked all day, so that the beach is the only alternative and, two, that I haven't told Jess any of this yet and she might tell me to go just where you figured she'd tell you to go. Understood?''

''I think I'm getting a headache,'' Ryan said, and, thanks to the marvels of telephone technology, Matt could clearly hear his friend's exasperated sigh more than one hundred miles away in Allentown. "Let's recap, shall we? Jess is pregnant—God, that one still does it to me! She knows *you know* she's pregnant. The two of you are getting married on Saturday, or at least you and Reverend Colter know you're getting married on Saturday, but you're not that sure Jess is going to show up to play the part of the blushing bride. Which—and I'm only making a wild stab at this, you understand—means she hates your guts. How am I doing so far?"

"Pretty good. Except you forgot to add that she hates your guts and Allie's guts, for telling me where she is and *how* she is."

Another pregnant—should he use that word, even in his head?—pause. Then Ryan said, "Well, it's been nice talking to you, Matt. Bye."

"Hey, wait a minute!" Matt shouted into the phone, then quickly turned his back to the smiling young woman in the skimpy yellow bikini who had looked at him hopefully, as if he had been speaking to her. "Wait a minute," he repeated quietly, wondering when it was that he had lost control of his mind, body and any slim belief that he was a competent person, a person with his head planted very squarely on his shoulders, a man who could actually walk and chew gum at the same time. "I need help, Ryan."

"You sure do," Ryan agreed, chuckling. "You know, I'm beginning to see the humor in this whole thing, which just goes to prove that even as I try to be a grown-up, Allie's influence must have corrupted me in some way. What do you want me to do?"

"I don't know," Matt admitted. "There's that old bit about safety in numbers, but I really think it would be best if you kept Allie and Maddy and anyone else as far from Ocean City as you can a while longer. Can you do that?"

"Remember that herd of wild horses analogy, Matt?"

Matt blew out his breath in a rush. "Yeah. Right. Okay, plan B."

"There's a plan B? Good."

"There isn't a plan B, Ryan, at least not on this end. I was hoping *you* had a plan B."

"Always the optimist, Matt, aren't you?" Ryan quipped, chuckling. "Look, why don't you just go with the flow, all right? You told Jess you know she's pregnant, you told her you love her—"

"I didn't tell her that second part yet," Matt admitted, looking up to see he had reached the small set of wooden stairs that led to the boardwalk at Brighton. "I can't tell her that one yet, because she'd probably hit me with something heavy. I mean, would *you* believe me? But I did get her to agree to marry me. She even gave me the name of your local church and pastor, so I could go out, make the arrangements."

If a pause were ever *pregnant,* this one was, and it went on for a long time. Finally, just as Matt felt sure the connection must have been broken, Ryan said, "She said yes, she told you the name of our pastor, and she sent you out to talk to him. And you think she's still back at the house, patiently waiting for you to return and continue running her life for her? You know, maybe we should think of spreading the Chandler banking money around a little—because you're out of your *tiny mind!*''

Matt was on the boardwalk now, running for the ramp that led down to Brighton on the land side of the boards. He could see the house, as it sat right on the beach. He could see the white walls, the green awnings. But he couldn't see Jess. She wasn't on the back porch. Still holding the phone to his ear, and not caring if he was breathing into it like some panting telephone stalker, he ran across the lawn and banged open the screen door. "Jess? Jessica!"

"Let me guess," Ryan said all the way from Allentown. "She's gone."

"I don't know," Matt answered, holding on to the phone like a lifeline as he ran through the house— the unlocked house, which gave him some small hope—and out the front door. He made a beeline for the garages, not taking another breath until he peered through the glass windows in the second garage and saw Jessica's car parked inside. "She...she's still here. Somewhere," he told Ryan.

"She is? Good. Sounds like you're still in the game. Now, tell you what I'm going to do, okay? I'm going to do my best to keep Allie and Maddy and whoever the hell else away from the beach house. If I manage that, you'll owe me, big-time. If I can't manage it, you'll know my broken and bloody body is lying somewhere in the old homestead, having been walked over by my entire family as they made for the limousine."

Matt nodded, already heading back toward the house. "Gotcha. And, Ryan?"

"Umm?"

"Thanks, friend. I already owe you big-time."

"Just tell me again that you love my sister, Matt."

"I love her more than I can reasonably feel free to tell her brother," he answered honestly. "I love her so much I'm stupid with it, clumsy with it, and if she doesn't kill me before Saturday, I'm going to spend the rest of my life proving that love to her."

"Damn, Matt, if that wasn't almost poetic. Now, do me a favor. Plug in that cell phone of yours and recharge the batteries so I can call you if I have to—either that or phone me twice a day. I think you need someone in your corner, your own private cheering section, and I've elected myself as captain of the cheerleading squad."

Matt closed his eyes, shook his head, nearly overcome by Ryan's friendship, the depth of it, his friend's willingness to say the hell with any gossip and scandal this quick wedding would set off and just be his friend. "Thanks, Ryan. And if you ever go off the deep end yourself, I'll be there for you. You can take that to the bank—preferably *my* bank."

"Not to worry, Matt. I'm the sane-and-sober Chandler, remember? I wouldn't know how to cause gossip *or* a scandal."

"You know, Ryan," Matt said just before they broke the connection, "I'm beginning to think that's a damn pity...."

Jessica slowly climbed out of sleep as she thought she heard her name being called out...first inquiringly, then with more urgency. Matt? Was Matt calling for her?

But then the voice stopped, and she lay back

against the pillows, rubbing at a crease in her cheek that was the result of having fallen asleep on top of the bedspread. Falling asleep when she had thought only to lie down for a few moments, gather her thoughts, try to figure out why she had been so quick to agree to this absurd marriage idea of Matt's in the first place.

She turned her head and squinted through the sunlight in order to read the printout of the digital clock beside the bed. Three o'clock? How had it become three o'clock, when she had only lain down for a few moments sometime before noon?

She knew the answer to that one, because she'd read all about it in one of the booklets she'd received from the obstetrics nurse after her initial visit with Dr. Fanon. Nausea, vomiting, bloated feelings, increased urge to urinate, mood swings, insomnia or fatigue—she'd been hit with every last symptom within days of reading about them. Whether this was the power of suggestion or she was to become the poster woman for the Inconveniences of Pregnancy, Jessica didn't know.

She did know that another seven months of this stuff could make a real conversation starter for her the first time she and her offspring attended some mothers with tots exercise program, or whatever that other pamphlet the nurse gave her described.

"One thing's for sure," she told her unborn child as she placed the palm of one hand on her stomach, "you are definitely showing all the signs of being your father's child. Rude, interrupting, pushy, barreling into my life and turning it upside-down."

Then she smiled as, in the way of pregnant women

everywhere, she felt herself getting misty over hearing those words aloud. *Your father's child.*

Matt's child. My child.

Our child.

Jessica felt tears stinging her eyes and didn't fight them, because these were happy tears.

So what if he didn't love her right now. He'd said they could be *happy*. And he was right. They could be happy. She'd make darn sure they were happy. And then, in time, he'd grow to love her, as she loved him, had always loved him. Wasn't she a great believer in happy endings?

The swing in her mood—her moods that swung so rapidly these days she felt she'd have to start using a scorecard to keep track of them—went from sentimental and hopeful to flustered and downright angry as she heard her name being called again.

"Jessica? Jess?" *Inquiringly.*

An edge now in Matt's voice as he called, "Jess? Damn it, Jess, where are you? Answer me. Your car is in the garage, and your purse is still in the kitchen, so I know you're here somewhere!"

He was taking inventory now? Checking up on her? Who did he think he was, anyway? Her *keeper?* The absolute *nerve* of the man! How *dare* he act as if he had a right to expect her to answer him, tell him where she was, *report* to him like some subordinate at his bank or something.

"I'm in here," she answered softly, so softly she barely heard herself say the words. Oh, she was being nasty, definitely. Nasty enough to be able to say that she'd answered him, he just hadn't heard her. "Right here, master," she ended, gritting her teeth, "come and find me."

And come and find her he did, after she'd stuffed a pillow over her mouth to keep from laughing out loud in a definitely unholy glee as she heard him opening and closing doors all up and down the second-floor hallway, each time calling "Jess?" into each empty room.

As his footsteps came nearer, she ditched the pillow, ran her fingers through her hair, and then lay back down carefully, rather *arranging* herself, with her head turned toward the windows, and feigned sleep.

"Jess? Are you in—oh," Matt said as he opened the right door at last, saw her lying on the bed.

She lay still for another moment, then stirred slowly, stretching out her long limbs as she turned onto her other side and opened her eyes. "Matt?" she asked sleepily. "Is something wrong? I was just taking a nap."

Oh, she was bad. Very, very bad. She could see the apprehension in his eyes, had heard the anxiety in his voice. He'd thought she'd gone, left, run from him. He really had thought that. And that thought had bothered him, really bothered him. Poor baby.

Suffer!

One hand still on the doorknob, Matt took another step into the room. "I'm sorry, Jess, I didn't mean to wake you. I just…I was out, seeing the minister…and then suddenly it occurred to me that you might have…that you might…well, that's all right, then, isn't it? Have you had lunch?"

"That I might have what, Matt?" Jessica asked as

she sat up, swung her long, bare legs over the side of her virginal twin bed in the room she had shared with Maddy for so many years. "That I might have packed my bags and left you here? Is that what you thought I might have done?"

And I might have, too, if I'd thought of it, she mused, *if I hadn't felt so tired and lain down to take a nap...and if it wasn't that I would have had to have been an* idiot *to leave a man who was out hunting up a minister and the Town Hall marriage bureau.*

Matt walked across the room, sat down beside her, pushed a thick lock of light brown hair behind her ear. "You've got a sleep face," he said, leaning across to kiss her cheek. "Funny, on you it looks good."

Jessica melted. Oh, how she wanted to hate him because she melted. But she couldn't help herself. He looked so sweet, he *was* so sweet. Which was pretty much how she'd gotten herself into this predicament in the first place.

Again she took refuge in anger and more than a little stubborn sarcasm, which wasn't at all like her. Although, just lately she'd been getting pretty good at both. "I'm already pregnant, Matt, and I've already agreed to marry you. So you can knock off the hearts-and-flowers stuff, okay? We made a bargain, that's all. And I'm not so sure I should have said yes."

"You're having second thoughts?"

No! "Yes."

"Yet you stayed, Jess. You could have gone, left town while I was away. But you didn't."

"I still could."

"Yes, but will you?"

She got up, put as much distance between them as she could without actually leaving the room. After all, it was *her* room. "I don't know," she answered honestly. "We'd be getting married for all the wrong reasons. Didn't you already try that, with Maddy? Look how that worked out—you didn't even get to the altar."

"But we have a child between us, Jess," Matt reminded her, then immediately wanted to kick himself. Of all the stupid things to say...

"Oh, that's right, I forgot. Hard to do, forget—when I'm tossing my cookies every two minutes and you remind me of it the minute in between." Words were lining up inside Jessica's head, nasty, cutting words she didn't examine before saying them; couldn't stop if she tried as they marched, quick-step toward her mouth. "Your child. Not me, not us—*your child.* You just proved my argument, Matt. Now go away, please. We don't want you, we don't need you. I don't want this huge *sacrifice* of yours on my conscience."

And, from the PEANUT GALLERY, another voice could be heard, saying, *Hey! Whoa! Speak for yourself, woman! I want him. I need him. Besides, so do you, Mom.*

Not that Jessica was feeling precisely psychic at that moment, able to listen to any "inside" voices, be they her own conscience or the pleadings and quite rational statements of her unborn child.

"I talked to Ryan a little while ago," Matt said then, completely throwing Jessica off with that verbal curve ball flying in from out of left field.

"You what? *Ryan?* Why?"

He stood up, scratched at his head just above his left ear, an endearing gesture to Jessica's mind's eye, not that she allowed herself to relax, enjoy it. "I'm still trying to figure that one out myself, Jess," he said, now adding that adorable grin to the head scratch, and nearly undermining all her fragile defenses.

One more mood swing, and she'd be going in circles!

Now because he was standing and suddenly the room she'd shared with Maddy seemed infinitely too small and the twin beds infinitely too large, Jess headed, barefoot, out into the hallway, sure Matt would follow.

As she marched toward the stairs, she said, "Is Ryan coming down here? Does he...does he *know?* Oh, God, what does it matter? Soon the whole world is going to know, aren't they?"

Matt caught up with her at the bottom of the steps, and they turned, together, down the hallway leading to the kitchen. "What is the whole world going to know, Jess? That we're married? That we're going to have a baby? Is that so bad? Do you really care all that much what other people think?"

She yanked open the refrigerator door and pulled out a pitcher of lemonade. Next came the slamming open of a cupboard door, the removal of two glasses that went *clunk* as they were deposited on the counter, the slamming shut of the cabinet door.

Then, as she didn't think she could stand without leaning her hands against the counter, she pressed down with both palms, bent her head as she gritted

out words she hadn't even known she'd been thinking, had *ever* thought:

"*Care?* What do I care? Do you mean, will I care
if people—anybody with the ability to count to nine
on their fingers—might think I *stole* you from my
baby sister a few days before her wedding? That, of
course, would be the people who aren't already thinking that Maddy dumped you to marry a fabulously
wealthy guy no one ever heard of before, of course.
No matter how you look at it, Matt, *you* come off the
injured innocent, and Maddy and I look like connivers
or fools or even worse, if there's anything worse anyone *can* think."

Matt took up the pitcher, poured them both a
drink—considering that Jessica had left the counter
and was now sitting in one of the kitchen chairs, her
arms crossed over her chest.

"So that's what Ryan meant," he said, half to himself. "Funny, I never really thought about all of that,
never really thought it through. I suppose I could just
say goodbye and good luck, and go home, leave you
to your disgrace? That is how you're seeing this pregnancy, isn't it? As some sort of social disgrace? Good
little Jessica Chandler. Perfect daughter, perfect businesswoman, perfect person—suddenly the talk of the
town, being whispered about behind her back?
Maddy? Maddy could care less, and we both know
it. Allie could care less. Even Ryan, who's pretty
straitlaced, couldn't care less, if I read him right during our call. It's *you,* Jess. Only *you* who is ashamed
of yourself, ashamed of what we did—ashamed of our
child."

Jessica looked up at him from beneath lowered eyelids. "Go to hell, Matthew," she said softly, all the anger gone, all the fight fled, all of her pain now coming to the surface, to shame her, to make her realize that she *had* been an idiot. She *had* been thinking these terrible things, if only subconsciously, and she hated herself—*hated herself*—as she saw all her jumbled thoughts held up in front of her for her inspection.

Suddenly she tensed, feeling the warmth of Matt's hands on her shoulders. Big, warm, forgiving hands; hands that had touched her before, had set her afire, then soothed her. Hands she could still feel, even when he was gone and all the light in her life went dark.

A dry sob racked her, and she couldn't help it that he felt her shoulders shake, that he'd heard her anguished cry, which said more than anything that had come before or that could be said now.

"What if I told you I love you, Jess, that I've loved you probably from the first moment I met you, that I've been an idiot and couldn't say the words and damn near ruined four lives because I didn't believe you could ever love me. What then, Jess?"

Jessica felt her head dropping lower, until her chin rested on her chest. "I...I wouldn't believe you," she whispered, then bit her bottom lip between her teeth to hold back the sob that was rising in her throat. "I *couldn't* believe you."

"No, of course you couldn't," Matt said, withdrawing his hands. "I shouldn't have mentioned it."

Jessica lifted one hand to her face, quickly swiped at a tear that had slipped from her eye and begun to roll down her cheek. "But thank you for trying, and for putting up with my irrational, near hysterics, which I promise are gone now,'' she heard herself say, and wondered if she'd entirely lost her mind. "That...that was really sweet of you. Honestly.''

"Yeah,'' Matt said hollowly. "It was real sweet of me.'' He stuck his hands in his pockets; he had to, because he wanted to touch her so much...so very much. "Okay. Okay. So I met with Reverend Colter, and the wedding will be on the beach, shortly after dawn this Saturday. But first we need the license, and we should go today, just in case there are any foul-ups in the system and the license is delayed. Are you up to a trip downtown? The offices close in about a half hour.''

Jessica nodded, not trusting her voice, and got up from the table, still with her head down, averted from Matt's sure-to-be-inquiring gaze. "Give me a few minutes, and I'll meet you outside, in front of the garages.''

She walked slowly up the stairs, still hugging herself, still telling herself it was no use crying over that cut-and-dried recital of their wedding plans. There was no use crying over anything, not anymore.

Not even over that very, very small hope of a happy ending she so irrationally still hugged close to her in the midst of so much unhappiness.

It's because she's pregnant, you know. I still haven't figured out Dad's excuse.
Not that I'll ever be that stubborn.
Wait a minute! I'm their kid, right? If they're stub-

born, it pretty much stands to reason that I'm going to be stubborn, too, right?

Boy, wait until the first time I don't want to go to bed.

That's going to be interesting!

Chapter Eight

Once upon a time Jessica had believed herself to be happy. She'd been eleven or twelve, or one of those ages that sees the future in rosy tones—one of those joyous moments before puberty and pimples and a size 34B bra, fiber filled, the politically correct term for *padded,* and being left home alone on prom night—where nothing is impossible.

Happy endings, for one.

But then her parents had died in that plane crash, and Jessica had, on her own, turned her back on childhood and decided that, as of that moment, she was no longer a child. Could not feel comfortable as a child.

She was Maddy's big sister, in charge of that little sister who played with dolls and still sucked her thumb sometimes in her sleep in the room they shared under the eaves in what Allie had always laughingly called the "hatchling nursery."

Allie was wonderful, Allie and Grandpop both. And, as Jessica's jet-setting parents hadn't been around much, anyway, it wasn't as if their loss had left some unfillable void in the lives of the Chandler children.

What it had left was a sense of obligation, something her father had never really taken seriously, much to Grandpop's disappointment.

Ryan had also felt the obligation. He hadn't ever sat down with Jessica and talked about it, but she knew how he felt. He'd gone to work during the summer vacations, including both high school and college, starting out on the very bottom rung at Chandler Industries—unloading materials on the truck dock— and then "up through the ranks."

Always a straight-A student, Ryan had become an A+ student, taking every possible extra-credit course in their progressive high school and graduating at the top of his class. Just as Jessica had, a few years later, graduated at the top of her class.

Ryan had gone on to nearby Lehigh University, living at home, not partaking in college life, and still working, working, working, at Chandler Industries. When Grandpop had died, Ryan had been right there, ready to step in, take over, at the ridiculously young age of twenty-three.

It had been much the same for Jessica. Good grades, commuting daily to Lehigh, work in the Chandler Industries offices and—when Ryan needed her, when Chandler Industries needed her—she had been right there, primed and ready to contribute her share, heft her part of the burden that came with running a huge, family-owned corporation.

They had been two very serious young people, more serious than Allie or Grandpop had wanted, definitely the opposite of their jet-setting, irresponsible parents.

Maddy, on the other hand, had been head majorette, junior prom queen, voted Most Likely To Marry the King of an Oil-Rich Country, and maintained, for her, a rock-solid-marvelous, straight-C report card all through high school, and an equally unimpressive grade-point average in college—where she had been president of her sorority and, yes, junior class queen.

Maddy was allowed her childhood, or she just took it, which was easy enough for her to do as, just as she'd said, she'd had no hope of topping either Ryan or Jessica, so why bother trying?

And Jessica did not begrudge Maddy a moment of her life, her easy popularity, her happiness, even her marvelous complexion, those huge green eyes in her heart-shaped face, or her size 36C—unlined!—bra cup shape.

When her sister had come home with her tail between her legs, looking so defeated after leaving Joe O'Malley standing alone outside that wedding chapel in Las Vegas, it had been Jessica who had held her while she cried, Jessica who had encouraged her to take the "domestic-oriented" classes at a local community college that seemed to bring her back to life.

It was Jessica who had smiled and hugged her when Maddy had announced her engagement to Matthew Garvey, then set about helping to plan "The Wedding of the Social Season."

Maddy's happy ending.

Except that was not what it had been, had it?

Maddy had "settled," which was something she'd never done before...and which probably explained why Jessica hadn't realized how unhappy her dear baby sister was until Joe O'Malley popped up on the scene a week before the wedding and turned everyone's lives upside-down.

Giving Maddy her *true* happy ending.

Leaving Jessica to think, to hope, to maybe see a chance...to dare to reach for her own happy ending.

Jessica turned onto her back in the virginal twin bed she'd slept in since childhood and stared up at the patterns a full moon traced on the ceiling.

"Well," she said, wiping away more of the stupid tears that just wouldn't stop falling, "that certainly was a self-serving trip down Memory Lane, wasn't it? Poor Jessica. Misunderstood Jessica." She wiped furiously at her wet cheeks. "Jessica the martyr. Jessica the good sister. Jessica the *jerk.*"

How long had she been in love with Matthew Garvey? Probably since the first time she'd walked into Ryan's office and been introduced to the sexily smiling, dark-haired, blue-eyed gentleman banker in the custom-designed suit that he wore so nonchalantly, as if he didn't realize that he stood before her wearing all the hallmarks of a minor god, at least in her mind.

She'd held out her hand, and he had taken it in his larger one, sending heat straight up her arm, setting off a battalion of butterflies that had been dozing somewhere in her romantic self, sound asleep, undisturbed, for all of her life until this moment.

Matt was Ryan's friend, Chandler Industries' banker, and he saw her as Ryan's sister, and the vice president of Chandler. Oh, he'd invited her out to dinner, but that was only because they worked together and, as an astute businessman, he knew the occasional dinner invitation to be good business.

Jessica refused to believe otherwise. That waylaid heartache, and she simply couldn't take the chance.

But then he'd begun coming to the house, wearing casual khakis and knit shirts, signaling that he was there as Ryan's friend and not as the head of the largest locally owned bank in all of eastern Pennsylvania. He played tennis with Allie. He watched Sunday-afternoon games on television with Ryan. He was invited to Christmas dinner, to Thanksgiving dinner, to all the many parties Allie seemed unable to live without.

In short, Matt became part of the family...but he never treated Jessica with less than the utmost respect, as if everyone else was "family" and she was still just the vice president. At least, that was how she saw it, unable to believe he could really, *really* be interested in her as a person.

Her years of burying herself in studies, in work, had made her an intelligent businesswoman, but she still had the social instincts and lack of courage of that same girl who had stayed home alone on prom night, writing an extra-credit book report on *The Grapes of Wrath*.

Jessica believed in what she could do as a part of Chandler Industries. She did not believe in herself as a woman.

It was that complex, that simple.

Maybe Matt did ask her out to dinner a few more times. Dinner or a movie or just to take a drive and look at the leaves doing their annual fall magic. But that was all it was, a courtesy to one of the daughters of the house, nothing more, and she had always politely declined. He was Ryan's friend.

Until Maddy had come home.

Maddy with her open ways, her huge smile, her easy laugh, her bouncy little body…her homemade chocolate brownies.

Maddy had no association with Chandler Industries. She was just Maddy. Sweet, adorable, *domestic* Maddy.

And Jessica retired even further to the sidelines, to watch, to marvel, as Matt and her sister laughed and went to dinner and danced at Allie's parties.

Slowly Maddy, who had come home so lost, so defeated, bloomed again. And Jessica had watched and wondered and mentally kicked herself for being so unlike Maddy, so much the opposite of everything Matthew Garvey seemed to want.

She threw back the covers and padded, barefoot, over to the window, gazing out at the ocean, looking at the silver path the moonlight cut through that ocean from horizon to shore. "This is good, Jess," she scolded herself as she blinked in the moonlight. "Now you're trying to pin a medal on yourself for being a good sister and to find excuses for going out to the gazebo that night to comfort Matt. Next you'll be telling yourself it was a purely unselfish action on your part to let him kiss you, hold you, make love to you…."

What if I told you I love you, Jess, that I've loved you probably from the first moment I met you, that I've been an idiot and couldn't say the words and

*damn near ruined four lives because I didn't believe
you could ever love me. What then, Jess?*

Jessica closed her eyes, wished Matt's earlier
words out of her mind, erased from her memory. He
couldn't have meant them. Could he?

Could he really have loved her from the beginning?
Loved her as she pushed him away, believing that he
saw her as part of Ryan, as part of Chandler Industries? And would she be a fool looking for heartbreak
if she ever thought otherwise?

Could he really have loved her after Maddy came
home? After the smiling, bubbly, wonderfully sweet
Maddy had been there to unwittingly show Jessica up
for just who she was—a too-thin, too-repressed, too-
career-oriented stick figure of a creature who could
talk for hours about facts and figures and inventories
and projections...but who couldn't hold a simple conversation on the weather or anything else without
showing herself to be gauche, untrained and definitely
not quite ready for a prime-time romantic relationship.

*What if I told you I love you, Jess, that I've loved
you probably from the first moment I met you, that
I've been an idiot and couldn't say the words and
damn near ruined four lives because I didn't believe
you could ever love me. What then, Jess?*

"Yes, what then, Jess?" she asked herself. "What
then?"

As had become her habit in only these few weeks,
she lowered a hand to her belly, pressed her palm
against the heat of her flesh as it all but burned
through her sheer nightgown.

"It would be so much easier if you weren't here,

you know," she whispered to her unborn child. "Then I could know if Matt really means what he told me, if he's been the same stupid idiot I've been all these years…if he really does love me, has loved me as long as I've loved him."

She sighed, turned back to the bed. "But you are here, aren't you? And you know what? I wouldn't change a thing, even if it would make my life easier right now, because I love you, sweet baby. I love you, and your daddy loves you, and for now that's enough, more than enough."

Jessica pulled the covers up over her again, placed both hands on her belly. "Oh, baby, what a whacking great load of gossip *you're* going to cause in a few months," she said, and then she laughed out loud, rather looking forward to, at last, this impromptu wedding Matt had threatened her with…to the words of love he had dared her with…and to the possible happy ending she had been too frightened to tease herself with.

Not that she was about to let *him* know that, she decided, still smarting over his sudden "revelation" that he had always loved her. *Sure*, he had. If she were to believe that, there was probably a bridge somewhere in Brooklyn somebody could sell her. He'd been lying to her earlier today, just so he could get her to the marriage license bureau before it closed. Nothing more than that.

But—and she hugged that *but* to her—that didn't mean he hadn't always *liked* her, now did it?

Why did she suddenly feel so…so *carefree?* So ready and willing to *play* with Matt a little between now and Saturday? Give him a little push, a small nudge in the direction of happily ever after, and see if he turned and ran—toward her or away from her.

What if I told you I love you, Jess?

If he did, he'd been as big an idiot all these years as she had been. They'd been a pair of idiots.

"Lucky you, baby," Jessica said, patting her belly. "That would leave you with a pair of idiots as your parents. Poor sweet baby. And I think *I* have problems!"

And then, against all reason, Jessica began to laugh.

Matt busied himself scrambling half a dozen eggs while bacon sizzled in another pan. He wondered, just for a moment, if the smell of the bacon would have Jessica descending on him in another few minutes, her stomach growling in anticipation...or if it would have the opposite effect, keeping her and her queasy stomach locked up tight, upstairs.

Well, it was too late to worry about that: the bacon was just about done, the eggs were fluffing up nicely, four pieces of wheat toast were staying warm wrapped in a terry cloth towel. The table was set, two tall glasses of orange juice were in place, and the three huge hydrangea blooms he'd cut from the garden hedge made a perfect centerpiece stuck into the vase he'd found on a top shelf.

Jessica's prenatal vitamins, which he'd stumbled over in a cabinet while looking for the vase, were placed beside her plate, just to show that, yes indeed, he was going to be a willing and helpful partner all through her pregnancy.

He was feeling quite domestic this morning, Matthew was, and he was very much delighted with himself.

It was amazing how much *hope* a man could find just by walking past a shut bedroom door after midnight and hearing a woman's laugh.

He'd really thought he'd blown it yesterday, telling Jessica that he loved her, had always loved her... even, his words had implied, as he had been heading toward the altar with her sister.

Jessica was right. Ryan was right. Tongues had to have been wagging back in Allentown when the Chandler-Garvey wedding had been called off at the last moment. Strangely, he'd really never considered the gossip, and none of it had reached him over the weeks, probably because he'd been labeled the jilted bridegroom, the poor sap, or whatever else a man gets called when his fiancée ditches him and then makes tabloid headlines by eloping with the latest software millionaire...possibly billionaire.

Oh, yeah, sure, he'd seen a couple of pitying looks at the club, but those hadn't bothered him. And he'd had more than a couple of phone calls from former girlfriends, casual dates he'd had over the years, squired to parties and concerts and that sort of thing.

He'd been the eligible bachelor back on the market, so to speak...so he'd really never given much thought to all this "scandal" and "gossip" Ryan had alluded to that Jessica seemed to cringe from in fear.

Now, just as everyone in their shared social set had probably found something else, someone else, to gossip about, he and Jessica were to get married...another Chandler-Garvey wedding to wave in front of Allentown society. Another wedding and, soon, a baby.

Jessica was worried, he knew. Ryan was busily pointing out that *he* had never had any sort of gossip attached to *his* name. Allie, who had pretty much set this whole mess in motion by bringing Joe O'Malley back on the scene, was probably rubbing her hands and cackling, enjoying herself very much.

Matt couldn't help himself. He laughed out loud, finding the whole thing to be, frankly, pretty damn funny. "Now if I can only get Jess to agree with me," he said aloud, sliding servings of scrambled eggs onto each of the plates already sitting on the table.

"Agree with you about what?" Jessica said, standing in the doorway between the hall and the kitchen and looking—Matt could see as he turned around in surprise—like her own special brand of summer sunshine.

She walked into the kitchen, her butter-yellow, sleeveless, knit top skimming her waist above a pair of short-short tennis whites that showed her long, slim, slightly tanned legs off in a way that nearly had the frying pan dropping out of Matt's suddenly nerveless hands.

But he recovered nicely. "Eggs," he said, pointing to the plates. "I was hoping I could get you to agree that scrambled eggs are better than over-easy eggs, especially for pregnant women. After all, you wouldn't want to take a chance on undercooked yolks, now would you?"

The moment the words were out of his mouth...and they came out of his mouth just as she was picking up the vitamin bottle with two fingers, as if it might bite her...Matt knew he'd said just the wrong thing. Again.

She waved the vitamin bottle in front of his face. "Just so you know, *Daddy,* I take these at night. For some reason, vitamins make me hungry all day, and I don't want to gain too much weight. We've settled on twenty-eight to thirty-three pounds, Dr. Fanon and I. If that's all right with you, you understand," she ended, before all but stomping over to the cabinet and depositing the pills inside on the bottom shelf.

Matt raced over to the stove, grabbing the bacon pan off the stove just before *crisp* could cross the line to *charred,* and drained the strips on a doubled-over piece of paper toweling. "I'm crossing another invisible line, aren't I, Jess?" he asked as he carried the bacon over to the table, placing two slices on her plate, three on his own.

She reached across the table, picked up a piece of bacon, ripped it in half and tossed one half back on his plate. "What makes you think that? You make breakfast without asking, set out my vitamins without asking, serve me the amount of eggs and bacon *you* think I should eat. Where would you ever get the idea that you might be interfering, Matt? I don't see it. I don't see it at all."

Matt unwrapped the toast and held out the plate to her before settling it on the table, beating down his impulse to place two pieces of the toast on the small plate beside her breakfast plate. "I never knew you to be sarcastic before, Jess. This is a whole new side of you."

She smiled at him, sweetly; so sweetly he had to know she wanted to murder him. "True, but you've *loved* me, Matt, remember? Loved me from the beginning, was it? And all without knowing that I just might be able to be sarcastic. In the words of somebody somewhere, 'Ain't love grand?'"

Matt raised his hands in front of him. "Okay, okay, I give up. I surrender. I'm still not quite sure what I did—"

"You told me you'd loved me from the moment—or was that the minute—you met me. You stood right here, right here in this kitchen, and said that to me yesterday, Matt."

"I did," he agreed, but warily, because obviously this was heading somewhere, and he didn't know where.

"Okay," Jessica said, picking up a piece of toast and nibbling on it as she spoke. "Prove it."

"Prove it?"

She sat back, dropped the toast onto the tabletop and wiped her hands as if to free them of crumbs. "That's right. *Prove it.*"

Matt looked left and right, as if this was some stage play he'd inadvertently gotten caught up in and there might be a prompter in one of the wings, ready to feed him his next line. "How...how in hell am I supposed to *prove* it, Jess? Either you believe me or you don't believe me."

Jessica couldn't believe how *good* she felt. She still wasn't quite sure *why* she felt so good, but it certainly was nice to see Matt squirm for a little bit, just as she had been squirming ever since he'd come to her the morning after they'd been together in the gazebo and *apologized* for making love to her.

"Gee, Matt, I guess you're right. It is rather hard

to prove, isn't it? Especially as Maddy would be Mrs. Matthew Garvey today if Joe hadn't come back.''

"Well," Matt interrupted, sighing. "I guess now that I've told you as much as I did, I probably should tell you the rest of it."

"The rest of it? The rest of what?"

"The rest of exactly *how* the wedding came to be called off," Matt told her, trying not to wince. He'd already figured out that Maddy hadn't confided in her that he had been as anxious to cancel the ceremony as she had been. That made sense, since Joe and Maddy had run off from the Chandler household that same night, eloped to Vegas and then gone straight on their extended honeymoon. Maddy probably hadn't had time to say much of anything to her sister…who had been out in the gazebo with the jilted groom at the time, come to think of it.

"You wouldn't dare," Jessica said softly, her lips compressed into a thin white line. "You wouldn't dare try to tell me that *you* were the one who called off the wedding. That's low, Matthew Garvey. That's really, really low."

Matt opened his mouth, trying to figure out how to explain the unexplainable, and then thought better of it. "Okay," he said instead. "We'll drop the subject. Eat your eggs, they're getting cold."

"I don't want to eat my eggs," Jessica told him, which wasn't exactly a fib, because her stomach had suddenly decided that buttered toast hadn't been such a good idea so soon after rising, and without so much as a glass of juice to "coat" her stomach, or whatever it might do. "And if I don't want to, I don't have to!"

Matt grinned, shook his head. "Mood swing," he said, knowing full well he was probably driving Jessica in the direction of actual mayhem. "I found a couple of books in the living room and spent the night boning up on the care and feeding of expectant mothers. This, Jess, is a mood swing, caused by your shuffling hormonal system. It's perfectly natural."

"Oh, it is, is it? Gee, maybe that explains why I'm getting this terrific mental image of you with scrambled eggs stuck to your stupid, grinning face!" she said, exploding from her chair and running out the back door.

Matt sat for a few moments, then picked up his fork. "She's crazy about me," he told himself bracingly. "One day at a time, one step at a time, this is all going to sort itself out. If," he added with a grimace, "she lets me live that long."

Good morning, everyone. Lovely day out here on the beach, isn't it? So, is anybody but me keeping score, here?

Mom loves Dad. Dad loves Mom.

Mom thinks Dad is handing her a bunch of...well, we all know what she thinks he's handing her.

Dad doesn't know Mom is head-over-heels crazy about him, and has been for a long, long time. That's probably because Mom's too afraid of the truth, and maybe a little ashamed that she never had the courage to go after the guy when he was available.

Which leaves us...where?

You know what? I think it's time for a little outside help, don't you?

Chapter Nine

Another day—and another—and still *nothing! Can you believe it?*

There's this saying, see...something about time flying when you're having fun. I heard it somewhere, I don't know where. Like I said, I know pretty much, even if they told me I won't remember it once I'm out of here and on my own. Why, I won't even be able to hold up my head by myself, if the stories I've heard are true.

But for now I can remember lots and lots. Like that business of time flying when you're having fun.

But, man, can it drag when you're not!

Mom thought she was on top of things there for a while, but Dad is playing his own games, too, I think. He's being nice to Mom, which is really getting to her, and she's trying not to be nice to him, which is getting to her even more.

She wants to believe he'd always loved her, and

she doesn't want to believe any such thing. She wants to tell him she's always loved him, but she's afraid he's lying and he'll think she's lying, too—or she's worried that if she tells the truth, she'll always have to wonder if he also told the whole truth.

I'm telling you, folks, a kid could get a headache!

Anyway, the days sure are dragging, with neither of them saying much to each other anymore, but we're getting closer to Saturday with every day. They'll have to start talking soon, especially if nobody comes along, like I've been hoping, to knock their heads together and get them to sit down and talk to each other for two minutes.

Parents. Can't live with 'em, can't live without 'em....

"So. Pick out any names yet?"

Jessica kept her head down, pretending to read her magazine, just as she had been pretending to read it for the past hour, ever since Matt had joined her on the back porch, sitting himself down across from her as if he'd been *invited* or something. Which he hadn't been...just as she hadn't even spoken to him for the past thirty-two hours and—she took a peek at her watch—twenty-six minutes.

Matt smiled a little, even waggled his eyebrows a little, only resisting crinkling up his nose in some Stan Laurel parody of perplexed idiocy—all while Jessica had her eyes downcast, and so only for his own benefit. He'd been given the cold-shoulder treatment since yesterday morning, and he was beginning to think he might be getting a little slap-happy.

"There's a listing of names in the back of that one

baby book I found in the living room. I've read it from cover to cover, considering that I haven't had much else to do."

Jessica lifted her gaze from her magazine, directing a look at him that told him most eloquently that she could think of something he could do—and that he wouldn't much like her suggestion.

"Yup," he pressed on, relaxing against the back of the chair, folding one calf across the other leg at the knee. "Cover to cover. In fact, if we get stranded in a snowstorm or something, and Junior decides to make his entrance, I know all about sterile water and boiling a shoelace to use to tie off the umbilical cord, and this neat thing about wrapping the baby in newspapers, if nothing else is handy, just to keep him—"

Without lifting her head, Jessica said, "How do you know it's going to be a boy?"

The moment the words were out of her mouth, she regretted breaking her silence. Because now he was going to talk to her again, probably talk her to death, and she had been doing so well...giving him the cold shoulder, keeping him off balance as she tried to figure out just what to do next. Considering that part of what she might have to do next was to admit to him that she had loved him the whole time he was engaged to Maddy and before that, had been enough to keep her teeth firmly clenched until now.

She might have been floating a little, just for a few hours the other day, when she'd decided it might be true, that Matt might have loved her—or, at the least, liked her a whole lot—even before he asked Maddy to marry him. She had, after all, never encouraged him, had she? He really, really could have loved her, then settled for Maddy when he believed true love was not in the cards for him.

Jessica rolled her eyes. Wow, what melodrama. She really should stop reading the crazy articles in this magazine. They were giving her all sorts of ideas, most of them pretty close to wacko, just like the article she'd read last night. What was the title of it again? Oh, yes. I Married My Husband's Best Friend.

Jessica closed the magazine, looked at the cover. Yes, it was one of Allie's magazines. Where *did* the woman find them? Although, she had to admit to herself, she had thoroughly enjoyed the romance novel she'd found in Allie's room. Everything had worked out for the characters in that book, and their troubles made her own look like a walk in the park on a lazy Sunday afternoon.

Of course, Jessica hadn't been captured by pirates, and Matt didn't have to fight off a half-dozen brigands with only a knife and a broken sword in order to save her.

Maybe they ought to consider themselves fortunate that all they had between them were some fibs, some stupid conclusions, a little gossip and their own stubborn pride.

Well, her pride. Matt was doing a pretty good job of being a really nice guy. She could kill him for that.

"... or David, which was my great-grandfather's name," Matt was saying, and Jessica realized she hadn't been paying attention.

"Huh?" she said, wondering why she had ever thought herself to be the least articulate, while she simultaneously contemplated just where she might have put her brain, then forgotten to retrieve it. "I mean...that is...David?"

"Not if you don't like it," Matt said, glad to see the spark back in Jessica's eyes. She seemed to "wander" around a lot lately, as if having private conversations he couldn't join. "I like the name Steve, but Steve Garvey was a big-time baseball player and that might be confusing."

"Stephen Armbruster sat behind me in third grade, and was always kicking the back of my desk. And once he stuck his bubble gum in my hair. There is *no* way I would name a child of mine Stephen. Besides, I want a girl."

Once more she wanted to slap herself on the forehead for speaking to him, even opening another line of conversation.

"The male determines the sex, Jessica," Matt said, watching with pleasure as a dusky pink tide rose in her cheeks. "It's true. I read it in the book. So, considering that *I* decide, I've decided it's a boy."

"That's *not* how it works!" Jessica all but exploded out of her chair and walked to the edge of the patio, to hold herself up by hanging on to the thick wooden pole. Her hands were shaking so badly she had to hold on to something, anything at all. "Sometimes I don't think I know you, Matt. You used to be so...so...so *rational.*"

"Hormones," Matt said, barely able to keep from laughing out loud.

Jessica whirled around to face him. "Hormones? Oh, really. And where in this book you've been reading is there anything about the *male* going through hormone changes?"

"It's called psychological pregnancy. Something like that. A concerned father, so I read, can actually begin to mimic his wife's—his *partner's*—symptoms. As a matter of fact, I think my stomach might have been a little bit upset this morning."

She glared icicles at him. "That's because you ate half the boardwalk last night," she said with some envy, as she'd seen the empty pizza box in the garbage this morning, along with a stick from a taffy apple, a paper cone from an extralarge serving of greasy French fries, and the wrapping from a take-home bag of cotton candy. She, on the other hand, had choked down cream of broccoli soup, stewed tomatoes and a pear. "And you only did it because you know I can't!"

Matt rose to his feet, took two steps in her direction. "Isn't this nice? We're talking again. Well, I'm talking. You're...well, Jess, you're sort of *screeching,* not that I would want to point that out to you."

"You just did," Jessica responded, backing up two steps, to keep distance between them. "Who *are* you? I thought I knew you. For five years I thought I knew you. Now, suddenly, you're acting like a cross between a circus clown and the village idiot. And I *don't* like it!"

"Yes, you do," Matt contradicted her, taking yet another step in her direction. "Or was that someone else who was in the kitchen yesterday morning, trying her best to drive me crazy, another someone in this house ever since I got here...running hot and cold, happy and said, angry and maybe just a little bit *receptive,* sometimes all at the same time?"

"I'm *pregnant!*" Jessica heard the words echo under the canvas roof and winced. What an absolutely *inane* thing to say!

"Yes, you are," Matt answered, bridging the rest of the gap between them. "And I'm in love with you."

She stood very still as he raised a hand, stroked her cheek. She closed her eyes as a tingle ran through her, from her cheek all the way down to her toes. "Don't," she pleaded, but very quietly, because otherwise he might hear her and obey her. He'd be like that, this new, confusing Matthew Garvey, picking the absolute one time she didn't want him to do as she pleaded.

"It's going to be all right, Jess," he breathed, his head coming closer, closer. "I know you feel something for me, or else you wouldn't have come to the gazebo that night, wouldn't have allowed...wouldn't have melted in my arms...wouldn't have let me do this," he said, brushing her mouth with his own, "...or this," he continued, his lips brushing the length of her throat even as his arms went around her, pulled her close against him, all along the length of him.

"Or this..." he ended, slanting his lips against hers again, not at all tentatively this time, but with heat, more than a hint of passion...yet with all the gentleness she could hope for, the kiss a tangible expression of emotions she wanted so much to believe he held; they shared.

Her arms went around him, awkwardly, jerkily, landing first on his shoulders, then slipping lower to his waist, where they remained, tightened, held on hard with the hope she'd never have to let go.

"Hey Mr. Gar-veeee! Whatcha doin', Mr. Gar-veeee, huh?"

Matt broke the kiss, saying something under his breath Jess couldn't hear but understood, anyway—the sentiments behind his words also hers. "Andy," he said, still holding on to Jessica, which was a good thing, because her knees had somehow forgotten how to hold her up. "And here comes the rest of our sand castle crew. And I'm willing to bet Jan isn't ready to talk to those three boys about the birds and the bees."

Jessica heard every other word now, still concentrating on recovering her breath, still wondering if her legs would support her. "I...I think I'll go inside, if you don't mind."

"Hey, Mr. Gar-veeee! Wanna come see my new pail and shovel? They're real neat!"

Matt put his hands on her shoulders, looked at her. "Are you okay?"

"A little wobbly," she admitted, which was all she would admit, could admit. This wasn't exactly the time or place for her to finally tell him that she'd loved him for years, had kept her silence for years. It certainly wasn't the time to tell him she still wondered if her trip to the gazebo had been one of friendly comforting, or if she'd had traces of a femme fatale in her somewhere who had actually gone to the gazebo to seduce her sister's ex-fiancé.

"I'll be fine."

Matt nodded, took a deep breath of his own. "I'd better go see Andy's new pail."

"Yes, you'd better," she agreed, then reached down inside herself and came up with a smile. "You're going to be a very good daddy, Matt." Then, before he could answer her, she turned and ran back into the house, to her room, telling herself she wouldn't leave it again until the next morning.

The sun was just barely over the horizon when Jessica, wide awake at dawn—as even a pregnant lady can't sleep for more than twelve hours at a stretch, she'd discovered—pulled the pancake mix from the pantry and sat it on the counter.

"'Just add water,'" she read, then read again, unable to believe anything could be that easy. There were even pictures on the box, showing the utensils she'd need, the temperature of the griddle, instructions on when to flip the pancake over.

Maddy could do this.

A child could do this.

A blindfolded child could do this.

She could do this.

Trying not to remind herself that she was about as domestic as her grandmother—which wasn't saying much—Jessica found an apron in one of the drawers, tied it around her waist. The ties went around her twice so that she tied the bow in the front, then looked down at the gingham thing with no little satisfaction. She still had her waistline. Bigger breasts, still with her small waist. Hey, things could be worse....

"Okay, stop stalling," she told herself out loud, then went on the hunt for the heavy griddle that replaced the two-burner module she'd already removed from the electric stovetop. She looked at the space left by removing the module.

"That can't be right," she said, then went hunting for the instruction booklet for the stove. Thank goodness someone in the Chandler family was domestic, she concluded, when she found the instruction booklets for all the kitchen appliances in a drawer beside the sink.

She looked at more pictures—if the entire "domestic world" came with pictures, she'd be a gourmet in no time—then went back to the pantry to unearth the heating coil that had to be plugged into the stove before she laid the griddle on top.

"Mission accomplished," she congratulated herself, then hunted up a large measuring cup, a mixing bowl, a whisk she remembered Maddy using once or twice, a large plastic ladle that looked about the right size.

She had college degrees, two of them. She could do this. Matthew wanted domestic? She'd give him domestic, in spades.

"Buttermilk pancakes, coming right up! Light, fluffy, melt-in-your-mouth pancakes," she said to the empty kitchen, taking a deep breath as she turned on the burners and then began measuring, pouring, mixing.

As the griddle heated, she took out the container of bacon and spread four strips at the back end of the griddle, figuring she'd kill two birds with one stone—and only have to wash that one stone after breakfast was served.

The table was already set; juice had been poured into two glasses she'd chilled in the freezer. A container of defrosted blueberries had been tipped into a bowl. She had maple syrup in another bowl, already to slip into the microwave for a few seconds to warm it.

Lordy, but she was good at this stuff!

She wet her fingers under the tap, then stood back and flicked her fingers in the direction of the griddle, double checking its heat, even though the bacon had begun to sizzle. So did the water, dancing in little balls as it hit the hot metal.

It was time.

Dipping the ladle into the batter—which was *supposed* to have some lumps, as it did—she carefully poured four small circles of batter on the griddle, then stood by, spatula in hand, to flip them when bubbles appeared in the middle of each and the edges of the pancakes looked ''dry.''

There was only one problem, but it was a problem she really couldn't ignore. Her stomach. It was doing a series of complicated flips inside her as the aroma of frying bacon suddenly had about the same appeal as having a skunk cross her path.

She swallowed. Swallowed again. Closed her eyes and begged. Nothing helped.

''Are those pancakes?'' Matt said as he walked into the kitchen. Did he have to show up now? Did he have to ask ''Are those pancakes?'' as if the idea of Jessica making breakfast was as expected as having come downstairs to see the London Philharmonic tuning up around the kitchen table.

''Take...take care of them,'' Jessica gritted out from between clenched teeth, then ran out of the room, heading for the powder room beside the laundry area.

She didn't have time to close the door behind her, which made it easy for Matt to come into the powder room after her, which was the *last* place she wanted him to be. "Get out," she ordered as she dropped to her knees in front of the commode, holding her arms tight against her roiling stomach.

"Not on your life," he said, and she closed her eyes as she felt the flat of his hand against her back, rubbing up and down her spine, stroking her, comforting her.

She began to rock, still clutching her stomach, still hoping the feeling would pass, that she wouldn't embarrass herself in front of him. Her eyes closed, her bottom lip held tightly between her teeth, she took deep breaths through her nose until her stomach, seemingly in a merciful mood this morning, slowly calmed.

She continued to take deep breaths through her nose even as she opened her eyes, turned to Matt to tell him she was all right. Except that last deep breath told her something...something he had to know. "The pancakes!" she yelled at him, nearly climbing him like a tree in her hurry to get to her feet. "The pancakes...the *bacon!*"

The fire alarm.

It went off as they raced back toward the kitchen...the kitchen that was rapidly filling with black smoke.

"I could have done it," Jessica said, for about the twentieth time in four hours, this time as she and Matt sat across from each other in a boardwalk restaurant, eating "light, fluffy" buttermilk pancakes topped with fresh blueberries. "If you had turned down the stove, *stayed* in the kitchen the way I told you to, I could have done it."

"No question," Matt said, trying not to grin at her, which would probably earn him a swift kick under the table. "It was my fault. All of it. The burned food, the fire alarm, the smoke—the hook-and-ladder truck that pulled up, the firemen running all over the place, the crowds coming down from the boardwalk to watch. All my fault. Definitely."

"I asked them not to use the siren," Jessica groused, her chin just about colliding with her chest. "The alarm company called, I told them there was no fire, just smoke. But, *no.* They had to send the fire company, just to make sure. Fine, send the fire truck. But *no* blaring sirens, okay? I asked them that *three times.*"

"Not a very obedient sort, firemen, when fire alarms go off," Matt said, trying to be fair. "I mean, those poor guys are all volunteers. Sitting around, playing cards, waiting for the fire bell to ring. Hours and hours, sometimes weeks and weeks, and nobody is considerate enough to set off their fire alarm. Is it any wonder they want to use the siren when they can?"

Jessica stared at him for long moments. "If I told you to go to hell, would you?"

Now Matt did grin. "Until the fans the firemen left behind for us get all that smoke out of the house, I could just go back there, couldn't I? Not quite the same as hell, but I could just pretend about the flames and pitchforks."

"Pay the check, funny man," Jessica ordered, getting up from the table before he could see her smile. He'd really been wonderful, not that she wanted to tell him so. He'd rescued the burned food before it could flame, tossing everything into the sink before turning off the stove and opening all the windows to let some of the smoke out.

He'd even had the presence of mind to close the old-fashioned swinging doors between the kitchen and the hallway, which had pretty much contained the smoke to the back of the house—the laundry area, powder room and a small, very "manly" study her grandfather had called his inner sanctum.

Jessica winced, remembering the sight of that room. They would probably have to have that huge stuffed sailfish over the mantel dry-cleaned or fumigated or whatever one did to turn it blue again....

Matt caught up to her on the boardwalk, and they dodged bicycles and pedal-surreys, joggers and in-line skaters, on their way back to the house.

"Still mad?" he asked after a while, taking her hand in his and giving it a squeeze.

"Only at myself," she admitted. "And we both still smell of smoke, even if we took showers after Smoky the Bear and friends finally left. I guess I just have to face it, Matt. I'm not Maddy. I'm not the least...domestic. Face it, Matt. I can't cook. I don't even *want* to cook."

He stopped, pulling her to a halt with him, and turned to face her. "Was that what this morning was all about? Jess?" he said, shaking his head. "That's nuts."

"But Maddy—" She stopped before she could say anything else.

"You're not Maddy, Jess," he said as they began walking again, carefully keeping to the area of the boardwalk designated for pedestrians. "Now, for the last time, Maddy and I were going to marry for all the wrong reasons, one of them being that she wanted to play house and I was looking for a traditional home, the sort I never had. But, in all that time, I loved you. *You*, Jess. I just thought you didn't want anything to do with marriage, that you were married to your career. So I screwed up, made a whopper of a mistake that, thankfully, wasn't permanent for either of us—any of us.''

Jessica kept walking, stepping around pouting pigeons, keeping her eyes on the boards, wishing everyone else in the world would just, for Pete's sake, *disappear* for a little while, so that she and Matt could settle this, once and for all.

''I know you hadn't planned on a baby, Jess. I know you love your job, a job you're damn good at—''

Now it was her turn to stop, pull him to a halt. ''Wrong. It's not that I don't want a child—children. It's that…it's that I just never thought I'd have any.'' She pulled her hand from his, wrapped her arms around her waist as she set off once more. ''I want this baby, Matt. I want this baby with all my heart. But…but somebody else is going to have to make pancakes for her, or else she'll probably starve to death.''

''*She?*''

They crossed the boards, dodging yet more human traffic, and headed down the ramp to Brighton. ''He. She. I don't care,'' Jessica said. ''I'm just so—*oh, no!*''

Jessica turned so quickly she bumped into Matt's

chest. "Come on, they're inside and couldn't have seen us. Let's make a run for it."

"Make a...*who* didn't see us?" Matt held on to Jessica's shoulders as he peered down the ramp, looked toward the house and saw the small, two-seater, red convertible sports car parked—or maybe *abandoned* would be a better word—in the driveway. "Allie," he said quietly. "Well, we knew it was too good to last...."

Allie? Did someone say Allie?

That would be my great-grandmother, right?

Hot-diggity! This could be just what we need!

This also ought to be fun, almost as much fun as listening to Mom explaining to the fireman about how the pancakes and bacon got burned. She blamed it all on me, of course.

That's going to cost her more than a few 2:00 a.m. feedings, let me tell you!

Now, if I can only stay awake long enough to find out what Grandma Allie is going to do. I'm sure those pancakes tasted good to Mom, but I think carbohydrates make me sleepy....

Chapter Ten

"Hello, darlings. I want to thank you for leaving the place intact, if a bit *smudged*."

"Allie," Jessica said carefully, kissing her grandmother on the cheek. "What are you doing here?"

"Answer your phone once in a while, and maybe I wouldn't be here. But after the alarm service called me—"

"What?" Jessica was suddenly livid. "How *dare* they call you!"

"It's in the contract, Jessica, as I'm the owner of record. They just wanted me to know the situation was under their control, and to be sure I'd allowed you and Matt to stay here, was aware of your presence." She sat back on the kitchen chair she'd covered with a cotton sheet and smiled at Matt. "Oh, I could have just phoned you—and I did, you didn't answer. But you all know Mrs. Ballantine. She wouldn't rest until she'd seen the place for herself."

"Mrs. Ballantine is here, too?" Jessica was amazed, more than amazed. "She actually rode down here in your sports car? With the top down? I don't believe it."

"She did whimper a time or two, especially when I passed this terribly *slow* truck on the Walt Whitman Bridge, but she's a trooper. And nosy as hell," she ended, grinning at Matt as Jessica stomped out of the room in a fine imitation of one of Maddy's temper tantrums—considering she had never had one herself, at least not until lately.

"She's looking well. A little flushed, but well."

Matt grinned back at Almira Chandler. "Go away, Allie."

"I beg your pardon?"

"No, you don't," Matt disagreed, still smiling. "You've never begged anyone's pardon, God love you. You're here to see how we're doing—how *I'm* doing. And I'll tell you, Allie. I'd be doing a whole lot better if you weren't here."

Allie stood up, smoothing down her khaki culotte skirt and adjusting her blue-and-white-flowered silk blouse. Even her casual clothes were all top of the line, and she wore them with a panache that would have greatly impressed their designers, who had probably drawn the patterns with a much younger woman in mind.

"Mrs. Ballantine is upstairs, unpacking," she informed Matt as she retrieved the ever-present pitcher of lemonade from the refrigerator. "I'm not here for the duration, whatever that would be, but I most definitely am here until I know what's going on. Ryan has been close as a clam, which isn't unusual. Jessica hasn't phoned me. Personally I see the call from the alarm company as a sign from Above, bringing me here to help you. You do need my help, don't you?''

"Would you be crushed if I said I didn't?"

"Not really, and I wouldn't believe you, either. Mrs. Ballantine has already told me that you and my granddaughter aren't sharing a room. Always were a slow starter, weren't you, Matt?''

He turned his back, stabbed his fingers through his hair. "I am *not* having this conversation with Jessica's grandmother. I can't be having this conversation with Jessica's grandmother.''

"Oh, Matt, lighten up. Or do you think I sent you down here to...to—goodness, I can't even *think* of another reason to have sent you down here. You're hero material, Matthew, I know you are. But you've got to use your *imagination,* get it in gear, get things going. I mean, I don't see any bouquets of flowers. I don't see a ring on my granddaughter's hand. I do not even see stars in her eyes. There should be stars in her eyes by now, Matthew.''

"Stars in the eyes are a little hard to come by, Allie, when she's throwing up every morning. But we're muddling through on our own, without any help from you, or any pointers, if you're going to start giving me orders now.''

"She loves you, Matthew.''

"No, she doesn't. She didn't even think about having children until this all happened to her. She loves her career, just like my sister, and—''

"Ah, yes, Linda," Allie interrupted. "Did I mention that she and Larry Barry are seeing each other almost nightly? No, I suppose I didn't. Joe says he's never seen his partner so confused, almost as if he can't add two and two anymore, and the man is a genius with numbers, according to Joe.''

Matt sat down on one of the still-soot-flaked chairs—it would seem that smoldering pancakes and burning bacon give off quite a shower of ash. Not that he noticed. He was too flabbergasted by Allie's statements. ''Linda? And Joe's business partner?'' He looked up at Allie, who smiled and nodded. ''Really? *Linda?*''

''You tend to put people in neat little boxes, don't you, Matthew?'' Allie asked rhetorically as she handed him a glass of lemonade and sat across from him at the table. ''I've noticed that about you. About Jessica, too. You decide who a person is, what a person is—and wants—and then you're utterly amazed when they don't act, or react, as you've decided they're programmed to do.''

''I do? I don't. I mean...do I?''

Allie reached across the table and patted his hand. ''Trust me on this one, Matt. You do. So does Jessica. You saw her as a career woman, with no time for romance, for marriage. She saw you as someone who couldn't possibly be interested in her, as she didn't fit what you—more often than you might believe—stated as your desires for your future. Little woman at home frying up the bacon, you bringing home that bacon—neither of you burning it. Big colonial house, like this one, white picket fence, tricycles in the driveway, at least two children, as you were born years after Linda, and didn't like growing up as an only child. Should I go on? I think I even know where you'd put the annual Christmas tree.''

"In the living room, in front of the bay window," Matt mumbled, wincing. "I didn't know I was so...so..."

"Traditional?" Allie interrupted happily. "Single-minded? *Bigmouthed?* I could go on. You're a sweet, wonderful, loving and caring soul, Matthew Garvey, but every word that came out of your mouth sent Jessica running from you, aware that she just didn't fit your image of the happy, domestic housewife and helpmate, or whatever "Brady Bunch" sitcom idea it is you have of marriage."

"I'm my own worst enemy, aren't I? Saying all those things, believing at least half of them? And all because I wanted to see how Jessica would react. She reacted all right—she never came near me." He stood up quickly, nearly tipping over the chair. "Go home, Allie. I've got even more explaining to do, and it might get a little loud. Jessica seems to have located her temper lately."

"Leave? We're supposed to leave?" Mrs. Ballantine entered the kitchen, a tall, almost rigid woman dressed in her usual black, although her hair looked slightly mussed, as even her severe bun probably couldn't stand up to a trip down the Atlantic City Expressway in Allie's two-seater convertible. "And who is going to clean up this mess, may I ask? The good housekeeping fairies? I doubt that, Mr. Garvey. I doubt that very much."

"Go get 'em, tiger," Allie said, laughing. "Stand back, Matt, I do believe Lucille is about to perform the miracle of the mop and rags. I have to see this. After all, as far as I can tell, she hasn't lifted a finger at Chandler House in fifteen years, other than to wag it in my face and tell me how flighty I am.''

Looking around the kitchen, at the summer snowstorm of black ash and the general grayness of the room, Matt at last relented. ''All right, but only overnight. We have to get ready for the wed—*damn!*''

Allie looked at Mrs. Ballantine and then at Matt, leaning forward in her chair. ''You have to get ready for the 'wed'? The 'wed'? Lucille, are you thinking what I'm thinking? Because I'm thinking there's going to be a wedding.''

Just as Allie was speaking, Jessica walked back into the room, now wearing a knee-length sunshine-yellow terry cloth robe tied snugly around her waist, her hair hanging loose and damp at her shoulders. Obviously she had taken yet another shower to rid her of any lingering smell of smoke.

She shot a look at her grandmother that Matt really didn't want to interpret, then glared at him as if he had just inadvertently pushed the button that would ignite World War III. ''I don't believe you,'' she said tightly. ''I leave you alone with her for ten minutes, and she knows everything we didn't want her to know. What did she use—thumbscrews? Or are you just a bigmouth?''

''See,'' Matt said, grinning at Allie. ''I told you. Temper. Definitely a temper.'' He deliberately lowered his voice. ''Hormones, you understand. They're on some sort of rampage. But they'll settle down soon, or at least they're supposed to settle down soon. Then the cravings start, I think.''

Jessica uttered something, some noise, that was somewhere between ''Ha!'' and a rather unladylike snort, then picked up Matt's glass of lemonade and drained it. "You were reading the Old Wives Tale section again. I'm burning that damn book, Garvey," she told him quietly, then said, "So she knows everything, right? The date, the time, the place? She probably even thinks it's romantic. We'll never get rid of her now."

"Don't talk about me as if I weren't here, young lady," Allie protested as Mrs. Ballantine, who had stomped out of the room, reentered, mop and pail in hand. "And I most certainly do know all about the ceremony, and I think it's more than romantic. It's almost poetic, something straight out of one of my beloved novels."

"You do, huh?" Jessica retorted, her hands now on her hips, her elbows all but flapping.

"Jess—" Matt warned, but it was too late, as Jessica was ignoring him.

"Dawn on the beach," she said, pressing on angrily. "It's so...so *contrived.*"

"Oh...Jess..." Matt persisted.

"And on such a busy morning, too," Allie said, her tone soft, commiserating.

Jessica nodded furiously. "Yes! Can you imagine how many people will be coming by—*gawking*—on a Saturday morning?" As Matt was now tapping her on the shoulder, she turned to glare at him. "What?"

"Too late, never mind," he said, then headed out of the room. "I think I'll take another shower while Allie explains it all to you. You might need another one, too, to cool off, after she tells you what you just did. The word *bigmouth* just might be in there somewhere, by the way."

"Take off your shoes before taking a step into that hallway, young man. I don't want anything tracked onto the carpets," Mrs. Ballantine called after him, which sort of ruined his great exit, as his sneakers were double knotted and he had to struggle to get out of them.

Jessica watched him go, telling herself he wasn't deserting her, that she really didn't need him here, to protect her from her own grandmother. Still, her gaze followed him until he was out of sight, and her deep, unconscious sigh did not exactly elude Allie's notice.

"You haven't told him, have you?" she asked as Mrs. Ballantine laid a clean dish towel on the chair and Jessica sat down across from her grandmother. "I didn't think you would."

Jessica shook her head, to clear it. "Tell him? Tell him what? He knows I'm pregnant, Allie. *You* took care of that, didn't you?"

"Yes, I did. I did a really good job of it, didn't I, Mrs. Ballantine? I told him. I am deducing—love that word, *deducing*—that he told you, and now you're getting married at dawn on Saturday, right down on the beach. I wish I could be here to see it, but you probably would rather I go somewhere else and stay there until the two of you have this settled."

"And you'd go?" Jessica asked, looking at her grandmother warily, because her grandmother never went peacefully, not when she had other plans.

"Only if you promise to tell him," Allie bargained as Mrs. Ballantine motioned for the two of them to get up, as she was about to wash the floor. "Come on, we'll continue this out on the porch."

Not knowing why she was being so obedient, but

glad to get away from the lingering smell of charred bacon and the new, harsh one of pine oil, Jessica followed Allie out onto the porch, then sat down, waiting for her grandmother to expound on whatever it was she insisted on talking about.

"You didn't tell him you love him, have loved him for years—that's what you haven't told him," Allie said, perching on the edge of one of the chairs and crossing one slim, seemingly ageless leg over the other. "I can't do it for you, you know."

Jessica hopped to her feet and began to pace. "I did not, I do not and I never did," she said with as much conviction as she could squeeze into her rather strained voice. "Maddy was engaged to him, Allie. Maddy was going to marry him. I was *not* in love with him. That would be...that would have been... and that night?...it would mean that I...that I *purposely*..."

Allie looked like, and purred like, the proverbial cat with canary feathers sticking out of the corner of her mouth. "Yes. Yes, it would, wouldn't it? And we always considered you to be the sane one, the shy and retiring one. Well, you know what they say about still waters, don't you, darling?"

Jessica collapsed into the chair she had so recently vacated, dropped her head into her hands. "Oh, I'm so *ashamed* of myself, Allie," she said, nearly moaning the words. "I did," she said then, lifting her head and looking straight at her grandmother. "I did love him. I think I've always loved him, even when I knew we weren't suited, even when I saw how well he and Maddy were suited for each other. How well I thought they were suited for each other, that is. And I did go out to the gazebo to check on Matt, to see how he was, to…to see if I couldn't make him see me…see *me*…."

"The Seduction of Matthew Garvey," Allie said, rising and coming over to put a hand on Jessica's shoulder. "Sounds like a great title to me, and a wonderful love story, if the two of you can get past whatever problems you think you have and *talk* to each other, *trust* each other just a little bit."

Jessica reached up, covered Allie's manicured, beringed hand with her own. "But there's more than just that. You heard the gossip after Maddy called off the wedding, Allie. We all did. Can you imagine what it's going to be like when everyone learns Matt and I are married—and then when our baby is born?"

Allie was silent for so long that Jessica looked up at her questioningly, surprised to see her usually happy grandmother looking about as angry as she'd ever seen her. "Jessica Marie Chandler, how *dare* you!" she exclaimed, backing up a step, removing her comforting hand. "Gossip? You're worried about *gossip?* You'd let what other people *think* dictate how you act, whether or not you're going to go after the happiness you and Matt deserve? Shame on you."

"Oh, God, you're right. You're right." Jessica's bottom lip began to tremble, and she had to sniff several times before she could speak. "I'm so sorry, Allie," she said, standing up and wrapping her arms around her grandmother. "For these past few weeks, since I've known about the baby, I've been so confused, lying awake, thinking about all sorts of silly things. Planning to be a single mother, wanting Matt so badly...and afraid. So afraid, all of the time. I guess I haven't been thinking clearly.''

"Matt loves you, darling," Allie said, stepping back in Jessica's embrace and looking up into her granddaughter's tear-streaked face. "He really does."

"He says he does. He even told me he's loved me for a long time," Jessica answered, trying to smile. "But since he knows about the baby..." Her voice trailed off, and she sighed yet again. "Timing, Allie. I guess it's all in the timing. I want to believe him, but at the same time, I can't believe he'll believe *me* if I were to tell him I've felt the same way, because if I didn't believe him because he said it so late, how would he believe me when I finally said it so late— if I hadn't believed him."

Allie chuckled. "You know, I'll bet you couldn't repeat that if you tried, but I think I understand what you're trying to say. And you know what? I think Matt will understand it, too, when you tell him. Mrs. Ballantine, we're not needed here!" she called out, heading for the screen door. "Pack it up, woman, we're getting the heck out of Dodge!"

"We're what? Leaving?" Mrs. Ballantine repeated, wringing out the mop in a large, blue plastic bucket. "But I've barely begun..."

Allie dismissed her protests with a wave of her hand. "Matt's a big boy. He can do it. And Jessica's pregnant, not an invalid. She can help, can't you, Jessica?"

Jessica nodded, still not believing her grandmother was actually going to decamp, leave and actually not interfere. It was...well, it was mind-boggling.

"Besides," Allie went on, taking the mop from

Mrs. Ballantine's nerveless fingers and handing it to Jessica. "I'm going to be a great-grandmother, you know. A daunting thought, Lucille, a daunting thought. I'm going to have to start thinking about making arrangements for that liposuction I've been considering."

Mrs. Ballantine pursed her red-red lips and rolled her eyes. "You're soon not going to remember what you really look like, if you haven't already forgotten. Don't you think enough is enough? Two face-lifts, the eye jobs, the forehead lift and whatever else you've done that I don't even want to think about. Young is how you feel, Almira, not how you look."

"Why, Lucille, I never realized you felt that way about my surgeries. I must say I'm impressed with your logic. Really. I must consider this. I am getting on in years, aren't I? Being a great-grandmother and all. Perhaps, just perhaps, it's time I stop *getting* stitches, and learn how to stitch samplers or crochet or some such thing."

Behind her Jessica discreetly coughed into her hand, trying and failing to get a mental image of her grandmother wielding a crochet hook.

"Silence, young lady," Allie warned, turning to Jessica, then picking up her designer straw bag and slinging it over her shoulder. "I can see it all now, Lucille. Great-grandma Allie. Crocheting, sipping tea. We'd be such good companions, Lucille, you and I. Talking about our bunions and our bladders and whatever else it is old ladies talk about."

Mrs. Ballantine stared at her employer and friend for long moments, then gave it up. "Never mind, forget I said anything. Get the liposuction. Let them take some fat from your fanny and inject it in your lips, I don't care. Just don't threaten me with bunions and bladders. I'll get our bags.''

''I thought you might see it my way,'' Allie called after Mrs. Ballantine, who was in such a hurry to get the overnight cases packed and back in the small trunk of the convertible that she forgot to remove her shoes before heading down the hallway.

''You're evil, Allie,'' Jessica said once they were alone. ''And I love you very much.''

''Of course you do, darling. Everybody loves me. As your grandfather said, I'm a very lovable person. As are you, my sweet, always-too-well-behaved-and-good grandchild. Now, if you promise *not* to behave, I'll leave here without a worry in my head. Which is a good thing, because you know how I dread frown lines.''

A quarter hour later, Matt and Jessica stood safely back on the grass, Matt's arm somehow coming to rest around Jessica's waist, as Allie and Mrs. Ballantine got ready to blast off on their way back to Allentown.

Allie wore mirrored aviator glasses and a jaunty baseball cap with her hair tucked up inside it, some of it hanging out of the small space between cap and adjustable strap in the back, just like a ponytail. She wore brown leather driving gloves with the knuckles cut out of them, and had tied a long white silk scarf around her neck.

Snoopy the World War II flying ace on speed, Matt thought, coughing to cover his laughter.

Mrs. Ballantine was also ready for the drive. She

had a black scarf tied around her head in true old-world fashion. She had a pair of vintage cat's-eyes, tortoiseshell sunglasses on her head—complete with straps attached to the ends, just in case the wind blew them off. She had a black cardigan pulled tight over her usual black skirt and blouse. She had adjusted her seat belt, twice. She had one hand braced against the dashboard and clutched a rosary in the other one.

Obviously, Mrs. Ballantine had traveled with Allie before and figured she needed all the help she could get.

"Toodle-oo, darlings, or whatever people say before going off on a road trip. Lucille and I had a small conference, and we're going to scoot back up the expressway—to exit nine, I think it is—and give ourselves a small holiday at Harrah's. There's some new bingo type slot machine there she's been dying to try out. Always humor the help, right, Lucille?"

"Shut up and drive, Almira," the housekeeper said, still staring straight ahead, as if expecting Allie to suddenly put the car in gear and crash it through the garage doors.

"Don't you just love Lucille, children? She's such a *happy* sort. All right, all right, we're off. We'll call you in a few days if we don't see you first. Please do everything I'd do," Allie suggested, then put the car in reverse and laid rubber as she backed out of the driveway.

"I wouldn't drive with that woman for a million dollars," Matt said, laughing out loud as they watched the little red sports car head down the street and disappear around the corner.

* * *

Maybe not you, Dad, but I can't wait! Vroooom-vroooom!

Now, what do you say you guys settle this thing so I can start thinking about some of the really important stuff. Like...I don't know...if child safety seats come with racing stripes...?

Chapter Eleven

For as happy as she'd been to see Allie and Mrs. Ballantine leave, Jessica found herself feeling more than a little daunted as she and Matt reentered the kitchen and looked at the half clean, half dirty mess the kitchen had become.

Half the counters were clean and shiny, half were still gray and dingy. Half the tile floor shone bright and clean, the other half still showed the marks of the firemen's boots as they'd gone traipsing through, placing the fans that still blew from each corner.

She shoved her hands onto her hips. "Looks like a split screen before-and-after picture, doesn't it? Where on earth do we start?"

Matt put his hands on Jessica's shoulders and turned her toward the hallway. "You don't," he told her. "You take a nap, and I'll finish up here. Pizza for dinner?" he suggested as she moved forward, not even bothering to protest. She was just too tired.

"As long as I don't have to have broccoli on it, you've got a deal," Jessica said, and then climbed the stairs, just about pulling herself up hand over hand on the banister, then collapsed on her bed.

Tonight, she decided just before she fell asleep. *I'll tell him tonight. This mom-to-be is a femme fatale, and she didn't even know it. Wonder what Matt will say when he figures out I seduced him....*

She woke suddenly to the sound of the telephone ringing beside her bed. "'Lo," she mumbled into the receiver, her eyes still closed, the last of a lovely dream in which she and Matt were standing on the beach at dawn, he in his bare feet, her with flowers in her hair, reluctantly fading from her mind. "'Oose this, whaddya want, and it'd better be good."

"Jessica? Is that *you?* Goodness, can that really be you?"

Jessica opened her eyes and looked at the bedside clock. Almost four. She'd slept for *hours.* And now, unless she was still dreaming, Maddy was yelling at her. "Maddy?" she asked, blinking several times to finish clearing her head.

"No, it's the queen of Sheba selling aluminum siding. *Of course* it's Maddy. How many sisters do you have? Are you all right, Jess?"

Jessica sat up on the bed, ran a hand through her hair. "Yes, yes, I'm fine, Maddy. I...I was just taking a nap. So, you're home? How was the honeymoon?"

"Never mind that, Jess," Maddy said quickly. "Joe and I were out all day. We found the most delightful wallpaper for the kitchen—all these vines and trellises and even a matching border. But never mind that. We got home, then came over here to show Allie the samples, and found this *note*. The house caught on fire, Jess? How did the house catch on fire?''

''Sparks from the garage?'' Jessica offered hollowly, remembering a snippet from an old joke. ''Never mind. There was *no* fire, Maddy, just a lot of smoke when something burned on the stove. Okay, maybe there were a few flames, just from the bacon. Flames…and maybe some floating ashes…and some water all over the floor because when Matt put the griddle in the sink and turned on the faucet, the water all but *jumped* off the hot griddle and landed on the floor, and so the firemen tracked dirt all over, and…but there was no reason for Allie to come down here.''

''Yeah, right. Like Allie was going to let such a great opportunity to snoop slip through her fingers. Glad to hear the house is intact—at least I think you said that. So, is that why you're napping? To escape Allie?''

''No, she's gone off to drive the staff nuts at Harrah's for a few days,'' Jessica said as she held the receiver to her ear and climbed out of the bed to walk across the room and examine her reflection in the mirror. She sighed deeply. ''Another sleep face. How do you be a femme fatale with a sleep face?''

''What? Jess, what are you talking about? Is Matt still there? Well, of course he is. Ryan says he won't come home until you do, and you're still there, aren't you? How…how is it going?''

Jessica could have asked something like, ''How is *what* going?'' or something equally inane, but she didn't bother. Between Allie and Ryan and knowing

Maddy's persistent ways, her baby sister had to know everything by now.

Well, almost everything.

"We're getting married on Saturday morning," Jessica said, then prudently held the receiver away before Maddy could squeal into her ear.

"Married! Joe, Jessica and Matt are getting married! Isn't that *wonderful!* Jess—Jess? Can we come down? Joe and me, that is. We could be your witnesses, or whatever, and then we'd go away, honest, and leave you alone, I promise. *Please,* Jess?"

Jessica blinked back quick tears. "You're not worried that the tongues will start wagging again, Maddy? I mean, two months ago Matt was going to be marrying you, remember?"

"Yeah," Maddy said in typical forthright Maddy manner, "but he didn't really want to. I never saw a guy so happy to be dumped."

"Happy," Jessica repeated, looking at her reflection, watching as the blood slowly drained from her face. "So it's true? It was...it was *mutual?*"

"Mutual? Jess, if I hadn't gone to Matt, he would have come to me. Haven't you figured it out yet? The man's in love with you. I know it now, Ryan knows it, Joe knows it. You're the only person in the world who wouldn't know it."

Jessica stepped back, sat down on the bottom of the bed. "I can believe him. He wasn't just trying to make me feel better."

"No, of course not, Jess. But I'm surprised he convinced you so soon. I mean, he was so sure you were all but married to your career, like his sister, Linda."

"You know, I keep hearing this. Who said I wanted a career instead of a husband and family?"

"You did, Jess," Maddy said. "Lots of times."

"I did?"

"Trust me, you did. Oh, maybe you didn't say *instead* of a husband and family. But you sure did make it clear you couldn't see the thrill I get from cooking and gardening and decorating and all that stuff."

"I talk too much," Jessica said, mostly to herself. "Then maybe it is true. Maybe he *was* in love with me before he heard about the baby."

"What? Jessica, did you say *baby?* I couldn't have heard you right. What baby?"

Pressing a hand to her mouth to stop her giggles, Jessica took a deep breath, then said, "Yes, Maddy, *baby*. Which is *why* I thought Matt came down here after me. I can't believe Allie didn't tell you. Why is it she learned to keep her mouth shut the one time I'd want her to save me from having to explain to everyone. Maddy, I seduced Matt the night you two called off your wedding. Honest to God, Maddy. I followed him out to the gazebo...and I seduced him. Me."

"And you got *pregnant?* Wow, Jess, when you break out of the mold, you don't go halfway, do you? Joe! I'm going to be an *aunt!* Isn't it wonderful?"

Jessica pulled the receiver away from her ear once more as Maddy yelled to her husband. She hadn't seen that one coming, and her ear would probably ring for ten minutes.

"Jess?"

"Hello, Joe," she said, as Joe O'Malley must have taken the phone from Maddy.

"Congratulations, Jess. To you and Matt both. Maddy would talk to you some more, but she's kind of busy right now, jumping up and down and grinning wide enough that I think I can see her wisdom teeth. They're cute as all hell, by the way, just like the rest of her. Look, we're coming down, if that's all right. Saturday? Jess? Maddy is chanting *Sat-ur-day, Sat-ur-day.* Is that the day? And we'll bring Ryan."

"Well...I—"

"Don't you dare say no, Jessica Chandler!" Maddy had grabbed the phone once more, obviously. "If I know Allie—and we *all* know Allie—she'll be there, and we're going to be there, too. Family should be together in happy times like this."

"You eloped to Vegas, Maddy," Jessica pointed out reasonably. "I didn't hear you asking us all to come along with you."

"Don't be picky," Maddy said, and Jessica could imagine her baby sister wrinkling up her nose and dismissing any piddling facts that didn't coincide with her own plans. "Saturday, Jess. When's the wedding—what time?"

Now Jessica did laugh. "Dawn," she said. "So sorry."

"She says dawn," Jessica heard Maddy telling Joe, then heard the rumble of his voice, although she couldn't make out what he was saying. "We can? We can really do that? Wow! Jess? Joe says we'll fly down by helicopter Friday night, stay in one of the casino hotels, stay up all night gambling...and other stuff...and then hire a limousine and meet you at the house early Saturday morning. Isn't that just *unbelievable?* I think I like being married to a very rich man. Luckily he's also cute as a button," she ended, then giggled as Jessica heard that manly growl yet again.

Shaking her head, and wondering how she was going to tell Matt that the beach was going to be even more crowded Saturday morning than either of them might have supposed, Jessica frowned as yet another thought hit her. "Maddy? What about Ryan, Maddy?"

"Ryan? What about him? He can come with us. I'm sure there's lots of room in a helicopter."

"No, no, that's not what I meant. I mean, what about Ryan, as in, do you think he's happy? I mean, he works as hard as I do at the office, and we pretty much are married to the job. I never told him I wanted more. You didn't tell me you still loved Joe. I never told you I love Matt. We're sure a closemouthed bunch for people who think we're pretty open and sharing. That leaves Ryan, Maddy. Quiet, hardworking Ryan. Do you think Ryan wants more?"

"I don't know, Jess. I guess we could ask him," Maddy said, "but right now I want to know more about you and Matt, if you don't mind. Are you really happy? Did he laugh or frown when you told him what Allie told me—that you've been in love with him for years? By the way, I'll forgive you for that someday. You really should have told me. But, as long as you've told Matt, I guess that's all right."

"I haven't told him," Jessica admitted, wincing.

Sure enough, Maddy's voice all but leaped through the wires yet again. "You haven't *told* him? Jess! What are you doing talking to me? You're getting married on Saturday to a man who loves you. Does he think you're marrying him only because you're pregnant?''

Jessica's eyes went wide as she stared at her reflection. "I...I hadn't thought about that. I was so busy worrying about explaining why I chased after him, why I...well, you know. And then I couldn't believe he really loved me, not since he already knew about the baby.''

"Uh-huh,'' Maddy said, suddenly sounding very grown-up. "You've spent the past two months this way, Jess? All tied up in knots and thinking in circles?''

"Not the whole two months,'' Jessica said, smiling sadly. "I worried about that night, yes, but I didn't really go crazy until the stick turned blue, if you must know. Am I crazy, Maddy?''

"No, my darling big sister, you're not. You're in love. Take it from me, we can do a lot of damage to ourselves when we try to rationalize our emotions. Now I'm going to tell you what you're going to do. You're going to say goodbye to me, hang up, and go find Matt. You're going to tell him you've been in love with him forever, you knew what you were doing when you followed him to the gazebo that night— God, Jess, the *gazebo!*—and that if he doesn't like it, well, he can just learn to live with it. I think he'll like it very much.''

Jessica stuck the tip of her thumb into her mouth, bit down on it for a second. "Yes,'' she said slowly. "I can do this. I mean, it sounds so *easy* now. Why did I make it all so hard?''

"Because you're pregnant?'' Maddy suggested.

Jessica took the receiver away from her ear and

glared at it for a moment before pressing it to her ear once more. "Are you *sure* you haven't been talking to Matt?" she asked, feeling just a little bit giddy.

"Jessica," Maddy said, sounding like Jess's third-grade teacher, Mrs. Biggs, who had made learning multiplication tables less than a joy, "hang up, go find Matt and tell him you love him. Honestly…some people's kids," she said with a chuckle. "Hey, see you Saturday, okay?"

"Okay," Jessica said, but she was speaking to a dial tone.

Feeling a little warm from her nap, and probably stalling for time, Jessica headed for the bathroom once more. This time she didn't take a shower. She took a bath. A bubble bath. A long, lingering soak in the tub, during which she played with the drip from the tap with her big toe, sang snatches of old songs…and grinned.

She grinned a lot.

Then, dressed in a snow-white cotton crop top and a pair of deep-purple cotton shorts, and with her sea-shore-curly hair tied back in a ponytail and her feet bare, she went downstairs in search of Matt.

She found him out in the side yard that abutted the living hydrangea fence, his hair still damp from his shower, passed out cold in the fisherman-net hammock. As she'd seen the kitchen on her way out, and the room seemed to almost sparkle in its cleanliness, she assumed he wasn't just catching a short nap; he was exhausted.

Poor baby. Poor, sweet, adorable baby. And wasn't it grand that he was so domestic….

"Matt?"

He didn't move, didn't stir.

She stepped closer and tried again. "Mr. Garvey? Wake up, Mr. Garvey. Ms. Chandler is here to tell you she loves you."

Then she stepped back quickly as Matt's eyes flew open and he sat up, before, in seeming slow-motion, he tipped straight out of the hammock and landed face-first in the freshly cut grass.

"Oh, I'm so sorry," Jessica said, except that she was laughing, and that sort of ruined the "poor baby" image she had considered only moments earlier. "Are you hurt?"

"Say it again," Matt ordered softly as he sat up, rubbing bits of grass off his nose.

"Are you hurt?"

Matt shook his head, waved his hands in front of him...and was momentarily diverted by the sight of Jessica's long, straight legs as they stood in front of him. He stood up, took a step in her direction. "No, not that. Back, back. Back up and start over, okay?"

Jessica never felt so free. Telling him, actually saying the words, was so very, very freeing. So *easy*. And the words got easier with repetition. "I said, I love you."

Matt's grin did that same neat knee-melting trick it had always done for her. "Say it again."

She rolled her eyes. "I love you, I've loved you for years, and if you and Maddy hadn't called off the wedding I'm 99 percent sure I'd have told her. *You* are another matter. I don't think I ever would have gotten the courage to tell *you*. But I have it now."

"You love me," Matt said, rubbing a hand across

his mouth, then circling it behind him to scrub at the back of his neck. "And you loved me before? Before the gazebo? Before you knew about the baby? All that time—all that time, Jess—you were loving me just as I've been loving you?"

"If you don't believe me—" Jessica said, stepping back a pace, suddenly unsure of herself again.

Matt grabbed her by the waist, lifted her up and spun her around before setting her down in front of him once more. "Jessica, you most wonderful woman," he said, grinning, "I'd believe you if you told me Elvis was in the kitchen. I'd believe you if you said you'd been to the moon before breakfast. I'd believe you if—"

She stepped forward, put her fingers over his mouth to shush him. "We could go to the moon before dinner, if you like," she said, then felt her eyes widen as she realized what she'd just said. "Um...that is, if...well, that surely did just jump out of my mouth, didn't it?"

"God, Jess, how I love you. Saturday can't come soon enough—but we've waited this long. Or am I being too romantic?"

Jessica smiled. "Darling Matt, you can never be *too* romantic."

Epilogue

The sun rose over the Atlantic at its usual time on Saturday morning, but not so that anyone would notice. The dawn came softly, wrapped in mist and clouds and with the promise of rain before many more hours passed.

The small group assembled on the shore. Maddy and Joe. Almira and Lucille Ballantine. Ryan and the minister.

And Matt and Jessica.

Matt had phoned Ryan and asked him to stop by his apartment, bring along his tuxedo. It didn't look half-bad, even if Ryan had forgotten his shoes so Matt was standing on the beach, barefoot, as he held hands with Jessica.

She looked wonderful. Dressed all in ivory, wearing the simple gown Allie had brought with her from a boutique in Atlantic City; her hair a riot of curls in the dampness, the handkerchief-lace skirt caressing her long legs with each soft breeze off the ocean.

They recited their vows as Mrs. Ballantine handed out tissues and umbrellas, then kissed under a warm mist as the sky began to open, blessing their union, their future, with clear, cleansing rain.

"Kiss her later, Matt," Allie said, tugging on his sleeve as he and Jessica slipped into their own private world where rain and Allie and the whole world disappeared. "It's going to pour any moment. Let's get back to the house for the wedding breakfast."

Matt looked over Jessica's shoulder as she pressed her head against his chest and told everyone, "You go on ahead. We'll be there in a few minutes. Jess and I—well, we like walking in the rain. Don't we, darling?"

They held hands and watched as the small wedding party, huddled under umbrellas, all but ran toward the boardwalk, then they smiled at each other and followed them. They walked slowly as the rain intensified, enjoying every moment of that walk, committed, heart and mind and soul, to walk together for the rest of their lives.

Hi. I've been sleeping a lot lately. So, how goes it? Anything interesting happening?

Yeah, well, I couldn't have missed much, right? I'll catch up, see how Mom and Dad are doing. I think they're doing pretty well, because Mom has been singing a lot. I like when she sings and when she laughs.

Right now, though, all I want to do is stretch a little... straighten out my arms and legs...wiggle my hey! Who are you? I thought I was alone in here. Have you been here all along? And sucking your thumb, too. Show-off! Well, just remember, sister, I'm in charge here, okay?

Two of us. Who could have known?

How about this—I'm not quite sure, but I think I'm smiling.

Son of a gun....

* * * * *

And then there was one....
Don't miss Allie's delightful matchmaking in
RAFFLING RYAN, *on sale November 2000 in*
Silhouette Romance, the next sparkling story
in THE CHANDLER'S REQUEST...
from New York Times *bestselling author*
Kasey Michaels.

#1 *New York Times* bestselling author

NORA ROBERTS

introduces the loyal and loving, tempestuous and tantalizing Stanislaski family.

Coming in November 2000:

The Stanislaski Brothers

Mikhail and Alex

Their immigrant roots and warm, supportive home had made Mikhail and Alex Stanislaski both strong and passionate. And their charm makes them irresistible....

And in February 2001, watch for

THE STANISLASKI SISTERS:

Natasha and Rachel

Available at your favorite retail outlet.

Silhouette invites you to come
back to Whitehorn, Montana...

MONTANA MAVERICKS

WED IN WHITEHORN—
12 BRAND-NEW stories that capture living
and loving beneath the Big Sky where legends
live on and love lasts forever!

M·M

And the adventure continues...

October 2000—
Marilyn Pappano *Big Sky Lawman* (#5)

November 2000—
Pat Warren *The Baby Quest* (#6)

December 2000—
Karen Hughes *It Happened One Wedding Night* (#7)

January 2001—
Pamela Toth *The Birth Mother* (#8)

More MONTANA MAVERICKS coming soon!

Available at your favorite retail outlet.

Where love comes alive™

You're not going to believe this offer!

In October and November 2000, buy any two Harlequin or Silhouette books and save $10.00 off future purchases, or buy any three and save $20.00 off future purchases!

Just fill out this form and attach 2 proofs of purchase (cash register receipts) from October and November 2000 books and Harlequin will send you a coupon booklet worth a total savings of $10.00 off future purchases of Harlequin and Silhouette books in 2001. Send us 3 proofs of purchase and we will send you a coupon booklet worth a total savings of $20.00 off future purchases.

Saving money has never been this easy.

I accept your offer! Please send me a coupon booklet:

Name: _____

Address: _____ City: _____

State/Prov.: _____ Zip/Postal Code: _____

Optional Survey!

In a typical month, how many Harlequin or Silhouette books would you buy <u>new</u> at retail stores?

☐ Less than 1   ☐ 1   ☐ 2   ☐ 3 to 4   ☐ 5+

Which of the following statements best describes how you <u>buy</u> Harlequin or Silhouette books? Choose one answer only that <u>best</u> describes you.

☐ I am a regular buyer and reader
☐ I am a regular reader but buy only occasionally
☐ I only buy and read for specific times of the year, e.g. vacations
☐ I subscribe through Reader Service but also buy at retail stores
☐ I mainly borrow and buy only occasionally
☐ I am an occasional buyer and reader

Which of the following statements best describes how you <u>choose</u> the Harlequin and Silhouette series books you buy <u>new</u> at retail stores? By "series," we mean books within a particular line, such as *Harlequin PRESENTS* or *Silhouette SPECIAL EDITION*. Choose one answer only that <u>best</u> describes you.

☐ I only buy books from my favorite series
☐ I generally buy books from my favorite series but also buy books from other series on occasion
☐ I buy some books from my favorite series but also buy from many other series regularly
☐ I buy all types of books depending on my mood and what I find interesting and have no favorite series

Please send this form, along with your cash register receipts as proofs of purchase, to:
In the U.S.: Harlequin Books, P.O. Box 9057, Buffalo, NY 14269
In Canada: Harlequin Books, P.O. Box 622, Fort Erie, Ontario L2A 5X3
(Allow 4-6 weeks for delivery) Offer expires December 31, 2000.   PHQ4002

SILHOUETTE *Romance*

COMING NEXT MONTH

#1480 HER HONOR-BOUND LAWMAN—Karen Rose Smith
Storkville, USA

He was tall, dark and older, and he took her in when she'd had no home…or identity. When Emma Douglas's memory returned, she believed she and Sheriff Tucker Malone could have a future. But would the honor-bound lawman she'd come to love accept her in his bed…and in his heart?

#1481 RAFFLING RYAN—Kasey Michaels
The Chandlers Request…

"*Sold for $2,000!*" With those words wealthy Ryan Chandler reluctantly became earthy Janna Monroe's "date" for a day. Though bachelors for auction seemed ludicrous to Ryan, even crazier was his sudden desire to ditch singlehood for this single mom!

#1482 THE MILLIONAIRE'S WAITRESS WIFE—Carolyn Zane
The Brubaker Brides

For heiress turned waitress Elizabeth Derovencourt, money equaled misery. But her family, not their fortune, mattered. So she visited her ailing grandmother…with a dirt-poor denim-clad cowboy in tow as her "husband." Only she hadn't banked on Dakota Brubaker's irresistible charm—or his millions!

#1483 THE DOCTOR'S MEDICINE WOMAN—Donna Clayton
Single Doctor Dads

Dr. Travis Westcott wanted to adopt twin Native American boys, which was why he welcomed medicine woman Diana Chapman into his home. But somehow the once-burned beauty made Travis want to propose *another* addition to his family: a wife!

#1484 THE THIRD KISS—Leanna Wilson

The first kiss was purely attraction. Brooke Watson and Matt Cutter didn't believe in lasting love. But everyone else did, particularly their nagging families, which was why Brooke agreed to play act the tycoon's beaming bride-to-be. Yet as a *real* wedding date loomed, was a happily-ever-after possible?

#1485 THE WEDDING LULLABY—Melissa McClone

Their marriage had lasted only one night. No problems, no heartache. But unexpectedly Laurel Worthington found herself expecting! When she told father-to-be Brett Matthews her news, he insisted they marry again. But Laurel wasn't about to settle for anything but the *real* golden ring….